SPIRIT/FALL

Book Two: Fall

BRENDAN LLOYD

ISBN: 978-1-923078-88-8
Published by Vivid Publishing
A division of Fontaine Publishing Group
P.O. Box 948, Fremantle
Western Australia 6959
www.vividpublishing.com.au

 A catalogue record for this
book is available from the
National Library of Australia

CONTENTS

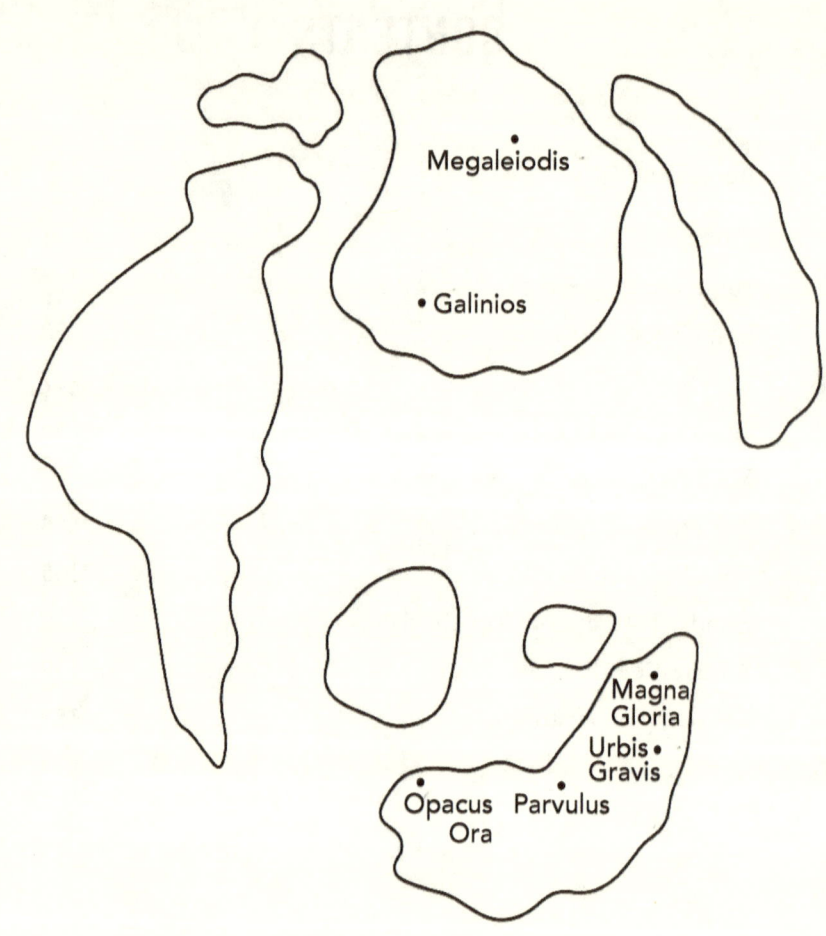

Megaleiodis

• Galinios

Magna
Gloria

Urbis •
Gravis

• Opacus   Parvulus
   Ora

BOOK TWO: FALL

PROLOGUE

667 U.C.E, Planet Asiyah – A time of great decline for the once mighty Verian Empire. Some thought the Verian Empire would last forever, but in the final years of its decline, the end came rather quickly indeed. The decline was more *moral* than *economic*.

The Verian Empire, guided…or perhaps *misguided* as the case may have been, by the teachings of the Imperial religion Sanctus never found peace with the Cetin for long.

A male Cetin possessing horns, a common enough occurrence, was often enough to spark almost literal demonisation – in that regard, the hornless female Cetin suffered less demonisation than the males, but suffered a different kind of demonisation: sexism.

While the Cetin might have had far more sinners than saints, at what point are the oppressed within their rights to oppose the oppressors?

In astronomical terms, Planet Asiyah might have been quite close to Planet Yetzirah, but in the 6th Century Universal Common Era, Planet Yetzirah might well have seemed a galaxy away. Contact between the two planets had not yet even been contemplated.

Contemplate, if you will, a less evolved time. Oppression might at some time or another been a way of life…perhaps, in a sense, it still *is*.

you." a voice said.

"My name is indeed Arundineus Vulgatus." Arundineus thought.

"Please step into the centre of the circle of sorcerers." The voice said.

"Will that not interrupt their summoning ritual?" Arundineus thought.

"Worry not about that. Simply step into the circle and hold your sword aloft." The voice said.

"What is *that* supposed to achieve?" Arundineus thought.

"You might be surprised." The voice said.

Arundineus squeezed between two of the sorcerers in the circle and stepped inside the circle.

"Arundineus, you will *ruin* the magic ceremony." Sors said.

"Maybe not." Arundineus said.

"This is highly unorthodox…I hope you know what you are doing." Sors said.

"So do *I*." Arundineus said.

In the centre of the circle, Arundineus brandished his sword and held it aloft.

"What are you trying to do, Arundineus?" Sors asked.

"All of us present might be surprised." Arundineus said.

"Surprised if raising his sword *achieved* anything, most likely." One of the sorcerers said.

Suddenly, a blue light appeared above the circle.

"Now, young Arundineus, I must ask you another favour – please leave the summoning circle." The voice said.

"'Summoning circle'...somehow I like the *sound* of that." Arundineus thought.

Arundineus left the circle of sorcerers. A being appearing much like a Roman Legionaire in black armour appeared in the centre of the circle. It had flaming blue mist coming out of its eyes and mouth, and was holding a red flaming blade and a blue tower shield.

"The spirit known as Legionaire! It was *not* simply a myth." Sors said.

"By what method did you perform that summoning?" Another of the sorcerers asked.

"'Method' would imply I knew exactly what I was doing." Arundineus said.

"Well, *powerful spirit*, are you strong enough as to kill a group as large as this circle of summon masters with a single movement of your sword?" Arundineus asked.

"Perhaps." Legionaire said.

"Well *perhaps* the Emperor would like to hear of your threat to kill this prestigious group of sorcerers?" Sors said.

"'Prestigious' is not a word *I* would have used to describe a group of sorcerers." Arundineus said.

"You were speaking *hypothetically*, I hope?" Sors said.

"How else can I get a vague idea of Legionaire's capabilities? There are no Cetin invading Parvulus   to test his abilities on. Unfortunately." Arundineus said.

"A lack of Cetin invaders is *unfortunate*? Why do we not

simply *ask them nicely* if they can invade Parvulus then?"
Sors said.

Arundineus, Sors and the sorcerers left the storehouse. Legionaire had disappeared. One of the sorcerers approached a house, where an unknown man approached him. The sorcerer gestured, and he and his unknown acquaintance retreated to a secluded location.

"Where are you, Legionaire? Why have you abandoned me?" Arundineus thought.

"I simply concealed myself. Would the average citizen be understanding if I were to literally walk beside you?" Legionaire said.

"I do not know any 'average citizens' that fear ghosts." Arundineus thought.

"Is a ghost what you believe me to be?" Legionaire asked.

"What else *could* you be? A *god*?" Arundineus thought.

Legionaire laughed.

"A god? Imaginative, I will give it *that*." Legionaire said.

"Have you stopped to contemplate the gods? It is not as strange as it sounds." Sors said.

"What makes you think it sounds strange?" Arundineus asked.

"*My* definition of strange might be different to yours." Sors answered.

"I was beginning to *contemplate* that possibility." Arundineus said.

"Let me know if you solve any mysteries about the gods." Sors said.

"How could I compete with your *prestigious* sorcerers?" Arundineus asked.

"Clearly you know something about the summoning arts my sorcerers do not. That is as much a mystery as the gods. I must bid you farewell." Sors answered.

Sors walked away.

"Would you like to contemplate the possibility of testing my capabilities?" Legionaire asked.

"There are no enemies nearby worthy of your capabilities." Arundineus thought.

"Would I be correct to assume the town of Parvulus is near a forest?" Legionaire asked.

"Why? Are there enemies in the forest?" Arundineus thought.

"Presumably, there would be *no one* in the forest, making it a suitable place for a demonstration." Legionaire said.

"The forest! Of course! I should have *thought* of that." Arundineus thought.

"The forests near Parvulus are not inhabited by any kind of native peoples, are they?" Legionaire asked.

"They might have been at *some* point." Arundineus thought.

"Do you expect the Verian Empire to be *honest* about the peoples it eliminates? Your official history is likely of dubious authenticity." Legionaire said.

"You are not to harm any native peoples, if any *are*

present in the forest." Arundineus thought.

"Please show me the way to the forest, young swordsman." Legionaire said.

"When I get to middle age, will you simply call me 'swordsman'? 'Middle age swordsman' hardly sounds respectable." Arundineus said.

"What makes you think being a *swordsman* is respectable?" Legionaire said.

Later that day, Arundineus entered the forest. He suddenly stopped walking.

"Is this far enough into the forest, summoned spirit?" Arundineus thought.

"Summoned spirit? I would tire of that phrase quickly. Can you please refer to me as an Animus?" Legionaire said.

"You answered my question with another question, *Animus*. In fact, you answered my question with *two* questions." Arundineus thought.

"It simply needs to be far enough into the forest that no townsfolk are at risk of injury from my demonstration. As a Chosen of the Empire, you must not endanger its citizens without good reason." Legionaire said.

"Chosen of the Empire? The Emperor had nothing to do with my ability to summon you." Arundineus thought.

"I said Chosen of the *Empire*, not Chosen of the *Emperor*. One may be said to be a Voice of the Many and the other, a Voice of the Few." Legionaire said.

"How am I to test your capabilities? Can you break a branch off a tree with your sword?" Arundineus asked.

"I am unsure what you are really asking. Are you asking if it is *possible* for me to break a branch off a tree with my sword, or are you asking if I *will* do it?" Legionaire answered.

"How was I in any way *unclear*?" Arundineus asked.

"That seems to be *unclear*." Legionaire answered.

"Slice a branch off a tree from a distance – is *that* clear enough?" Arundineus said.

Legionaire raised his sword and swung. A shockwave seemed to travel from the tip of his sword to a branch in a nearby tree, and severed the branch easily. Legionaire extended his free hand and the severed branch floated towards him. He grabbed the branch and held it high.

"Did you also want me to present the branch to you as proof?" Legionaire asked.

"You figured *that* out on your own but not that *other* thing? How did *that* manage to make more *sense* to you?" Arundineus said.

"Shall I discard this branch, or does that instruction not make enough *sense*?" Legionaire asked.

"What does not make sense is your sudden attitude." Arundineus answered.

"It would make sense if you got to know me." Legionaire said.

Legionaire used telekinesis to throw the branch to a space to his left.

"What else can you do?" Arundineus asked.

"Actually, my range of functions include…" Legionaire answered.

"Taking too many things *literally*, apparently. What functions do you have in battle?" Arundineus said.

"I could tell you or I could show you. Telling is not as fun, though." Legionaire said.

"Who said anything about *fun*? Can we settle for something between boredom and fun?" Arundineus asked.

"Mild amusement it is, then!" Legionaire answered.

"Does that ranged attack have a name?" Arundineus asked.

"Why, does it *need* one?" Legionaire answered.

"It might make it handy if I needed to use it in battle." Arundineus said.

"If *we* needed to use it in battle, you mean." Legionaire said.

"Is 'Empire Slash' too boring of a name for that attack you broke off that branch with?" Arundineus asked.

"Empire Slash!" Legionaire said.

Legionaire again used the same attack he used to sever the branch from a tree.

"Not too boring *at all*." Legionaire said.

"What about close combat?" Arundineus asked.

"What *about* it?" Legionaire answered.

"In battle, what should I call out to signify an ordinary slash of your sword?" Arundineus asked.

"Neither my sword nor its slashes are 'ordinary'." Legionaire said.

"Practice your sword skills on another tree." Arundineus said.

Legionaire hovered toward a different tree and sliced it horizontally, causing the tree to fall.

Arundineus held a hand near his chin.

"How about 'Empire Slice'?" Arundineus asked.

"Have you not considered the possibility of a *vertical* sword attack?" Legionaire answered.

"Why? Does a vertical attack do more damage?" Arundineus said.

"Never mind. The combination of Empire Slash and Empire Slice will likely suffice for most combat situations." Legionaire said.

"Do you have any kind of *defensive* functions?" Arundineus said.

"That is a rather *vague* question, would you not agree?"

"Ah! Then your defensive functions include *evading questions*?" Arundineus said.

"*Do* they?" Legionaire said.

"It was only amusing the *first* time." Arundineus said.

Suddenly, Legionaire flew toward a distant tree. Arundineus followed without hesitation. Legionaire pointed to a branch of the tree, where a man released a messenger bird.

"My defensive functions *also* include *exposing spies*." Legionaire said.

"Do not waste your time travelling to the capital unless you happen to possess a cure for insomnia." The spy said.

"I am sure I have no idea what you are talking about." Arundineus said.

"Lucky for *us*, then. You will not even see us coming." The spy said.

"And you will not even see the next sunrise. Kill the spy however you want." Arundineus said.

"Empire Thrust!" Legionaire said.

Legionaire stabbed the spy, and dispatched him easily.

"How did you figure all that out from 'kill the spy'?" Arundineus asked.

"The instruction 'kill' means much more than you think." Legionaire answered.

"How do *you* know how much I think?" Arundineus said.

Later that day, Arundineus re-entered Parvulus. Legionaire reappeared. A man with scruffy hair approached Arundineus.

"What battlefield did you *find* him on?" The scruffy-haired man said.

"Caelifer. The gods are being *generous*. Can we spar for a moment?" Arundineus said.

"The gods being generous, you say? My theory is that the gods would be more generous if they got more credit for their generosity. Think about it: they get too much credit for their cruelty and too little for their generosity. Why would the gods go out of their way to show generosity?" Caelifer said.

"Maybe to defy our expectations of them?" Arundineus said.

"*Your* theory is that the gods react to our *expectations* of them? I wonder if it can be proven." Caelifer said.

"Do you know a place suitable for sparring?" Arundineus asked.

"I know a few such places near Parvulus. Because you mentioned *generosity*, I will even show you the way there." Caelifer answered.

Legionaire disappeared. A little later, Caelifer led Arundineus to a mostly empty field behind the storehouse. Legionaire reappeared.

"Legionaire, because Caelifer is a friend, no serious harm is to come to him – do you understand?" Arundineus said.

"Who is going to decide what kind of harm counts as serious? Deus Benevolus guide you!" Caelifer said.

"No enduring harm is to befall young Caelifer. Very well, perhaps this sparring session might serve as an opportunity to be introduced to my defensive functions." Legionaire said.

"Am I supposed to be able to hear him like *you* do? I might have thought a *defensive function* would be making sure only the one who *summoned* you can see and hear you." Caelifer said.

"Were I to do that, the likelihood of *serious harm* befalling you would greatly increase." Legionaire said.

Caelifer brandished a two-handed sword.

"Two hands – twice as deadly." Caelifer said.

"And half as well defended without a shield." Arundineus said.

"Your friend Caelifer may unleash as many blows as he wishes. Arundineus, simply follow my instructions if you wish to greatly reduce the chances of being seriously harmed."

Caelifer rushed at Arundineus. Caelifer came within sword-strike range.

"Now, Arundineus, simply utter 'Shield of the Legion.'" Legionaire said.

"Shield of the Legion!" Arundineus said.

A spherical magical shield appeared around Arundineus. Caelifer attacked relentlessly but the integrity of the shield was unaffected. Caelifer began breathing heavily.

"Maybe one-on-one, you might exhaust an opponent, but you cannot defeat an army on your own." Caelifer said.

"Hopefully I will never *need* to. The gods cannot expect one man and his ghostly warrior to win against an army." Arundineus said.

"It was 'powerful spirit' before, now it is 'ghostly warrior'? Do I dare to ponder what it will be *next*?" Legionaire said.

"'Powerful spirit'? What is *that* about?" Caelifer asked.

"Never mind. Legionaire, is your demonstration complete?" Arundineus said.

"There are *other* functions I would familiarise you with." Legionaire said.

"Functions such as?" Arundineus asked.

"Attack Caelifer, but before you trade blows, utter 'Defender of the Legion.'" Legionaire said.

"Who gave him permission to attack me?!" Caelifer said.

"If your attacks connect before you have uttered the correct phrase, well, my condolences to any friends of young

Caelifer." Legionaire said.

"It would take more than that to kill 'young Caelifer.'" Caelifer said.

"So we should hope." Legionaire said.

Arundineus charged toward Caelifer.

"I hope you know what you are doing." Arundineus said.

"The feeling is mutual, I assure you." Legionaire said.

Arundineus closed in on Caelifer.

"Defender of the Legion!" Arundineus said.

A magical shield similar to the one that earlier surrounded Arundineus appeared surrounding Caelifer. Arundineus's charge collided with the magical shield, which withstood it.

"My condolences for anyone who happens to *hate* young Caelifer." Legionaire said.

"Why should anyone except the gods care about *them*?" Caelifer said.

"Defender of the Legion is not so different than *Shield* of the Legion." Arundineus said.

"Wait. Do you mean you failed to notice one must have inspired the other? Yet *you* are his master? The gods must be trying to be ironic about justice. Yes, *that* must be it." Caelifer said.

"Of course – the gods, those ancient masters of irony. Who could forget?" Legionaire said.

"For *him*, that actually counts as humour." Arundineus said.

"What is next for the prestigious spirit summoner?" Caelifer asked.

"A spy hinted at something that will happen in the capital. Do you know anything about a cure for insomnia?" Arundineus said.

"I know at least *one* cure for insomnia. Can I join you?" Caelifer said.

"Danger does not bother you?" Arundineus said.

"I would *laugh* in the face of danger…if danger actually had a face." Caelifer said.

"Death is not the worst thing that could happen to him." Legionaire said.

"Let us hope we never learn what things could be worse than death." Arundineus said.

"Already too late for *some*." Legionaire said.

"Caelifer, if you can find a good horse, meet me at the entrance to Parvulus." Arundineus said.

"Where are *you* going to find a good horse?" Caelifer said.

"Where would I find *bad* horses?" Arundineus said.

The next day, Arundineus and Caelifer, both on horseback, waited at the entrance to Parvulus. Legionaire was not present. Their horses started trotting away from Parvulus at a gentle pace.

"Not even the Cetin would dare attack Magna Gloria directly." Caelifer said.

"The spy could have been working for anyone. Perhaps even rebels." Arundineus said.

"So the spy did not look Cetin?" Caelifer asked.

"How would looking Cetin be helpful for a spy? They

would stand out anywhere there was not something green to camouflage them." Arundineus said.

"I suppose you are correct - never fight Cetin anywhere with long grass or in a forest, then, I guess. Are Cetin spies kidnapped then? Surely the Cetin are baby-stealers at least?" Caelifer asked.

"I suspect most Cetin spies are simply traitors who would spit on the notion of loyalty to the empire…loyal to whatever lines their coffers." Arundineus said.

"Does it work in reverse? Do we kidnap *Cetin* babies to spy on the *Cetin*?" Caelifer said.

"If *we* have measures to identity spies, so would *they*." Arundineus said.

"There goes any hope of the empire planning mass Cetin kidnappings to start a spy network. An idea too good to waste, *that* is." Caelifer said.

"An idea too good to be true, more like." Arundineus said.

A carrier pigeon swooped past Arundineus towards Parvulus.

"Did the spy have to wait *that* long for a response?" Caelifer said.

"The spy is dead. That might be an *imperial* pigeon." Arundineus said.

"Parvulus providing reinforcements for the capital? Parvulus is barely worth including on a map." Caelifer said.

"Maybe Magna Gloria needs all the reinforcements it can muster." Arundineus said.

"Or, a merchant wants to know what items are popular somewhere outside Parvulus." Caelifer said.

"A merchant would make a slow trade in a town as small as Parvulus." Arundineus said.

"Should we follow the pigeon and read the message it is delivering?" Caelifer said.

"Reading someone else's private messages should be a crime." Arundineus said.

LEST UNREST KNOW BEST

Arundineus and Caelifer arrived at the outskirts of the capital. There were no obvious signs of distress.

"Apparently, whoever the enemy is seems to not be in any kind of hurry." Arundineus said.

Legionaire reappeared.

"Perhaps the spy was deceiving you." Legionaire said.

"What did he mean we would not see them coming?" Arundineus asked.

"Why not simply summon his ghost and ask him?" Legionaire said.

"How do I summon a ghost when I do not even know their name?" Arundineus said.

"Anyone would think you had trouble summoning *me*." Legionaire said.

Suddenly, a magical aura appeared around Legionaire.

"No, I will not…" Legionaire said.

Legionaire seemed to fly towards the centre of the capital as though against his will.

"Will not bother to finish that sentence, apparently." Caelifer said.

"Have you known Legionaire to leave sentences unfinished?" Arundineus asked.

"What do we do? Charge into the capital and tell people to evacuate?" Caelifer said.

"Our horses will at some point be a hindrance." Arundineus said.

"Sell the horses and find some way of raising an alarm." Caelifer said.

"They do not seem to design Verian cities with ease of access by horse in mind, *do* they?" Arundineus said.

Later that day, without their horses, Arundineus and Caelifer entered deeper into the capital. There was an impressive citadel nearby where an ornately dressed man was in front of a large group of legionnaires.

"The capital may be in danger soon." Arundineus said.

"Did anyone manage to hear what he said?" The Verian Emperor said.

One legionnaire close to Arundineus and Caelifer approached the Emperor.

"He said the capital may be in danger soon." The Legionnaire said.

"How could he possibly have information the Verian Emperor himself does not? Does he have *proof*?" The Verian Emperor said.

The legionnaire ran back to Arundineus and Caelifer.

"Do you have proof about the danger to the capital?" The Legionnaire asked.

"You will get a decent amount of *athletic training* if *this* keeps up." Caelifer said.

"Should I have asked the spy I found to make copies of his secret message? Too late – he is already dead." Arundineus said.

"I will relay your response to Emperor Colubrifer." The Legionnaire said.

The legionnaire ran back to the emperor, stopped in front of him, and bowed.

"The spy who informed him of the threat to the capital is dead." The Legionnaire said.

"Am I to trust hearsay?" Emperor Colubrifer said.

"What message am I to relay to him?" The Legionnaire asked.

"This running back and forth nonsense grows tiresome. Bring them *here*." Emperor Colubrifer said.

The legionnaire ran back to Arundineus and Caelifer.

"Our Esteemed Emperor Cincinnatus Colubrifer has offered you an audience." The Legionnaire said.

"Look around. He does not need to worry about *finding an audience*, does he?" Caelifer said.

The legionnaire led Arundineus and Caelifer to the Verian Emperor.

"I do not make it my business to trust hearsay." Emperor Colubrifer said.

"When it comes to the *gods*, all we *have* is hearsay." Caelifer said.

"Perhaps. If I could only read your mind, young..."

Emperor Colubrifer said.

"Arundineus Vulgatus, and *he* is Caelifer Credo." Arundineus said.

"Arundineus Vulgatus…a true commoner. If I could only read your mind, I would know if you are even telling the truth about the threat to the capital." Emperor Colubrifer said.

"Did you see a legionnaire floating anywhere near here?" Arundineus asked.

"Have I seen a *legionnaire*? You will need to be more *specific*." Emperor Colubrifer answered.

"A floating legionnaire is not *specific* enough?" Arundineus said.

"Emperor Colubrifer, Arundineus said the spy who told him about the threat to the capital is already dead." The Legionnaire said.

"Did you not consider pleasing me by offering me the spy for questioning instead of offering me disappointment?" Emperor Colubrifer said.

"How do you offer someone *disappointment*? What sane person would *accept* that offer?" Caelifer said.

"I could easily offer you a *prison sentence* were I to be offended in any way." Emperor Colubrifer said.

"Please, remember Deus Benevolus." Caelifer said.

"If *he* is so benevolent, I do not see why *I* need to be." Emperor Colubrifer said.

Suddenly, a figure emerged atop a balcony of the citadel. He had green skin, pointed ears, yellow eyes, white hair, and horns as straight as daggers.

"Neither do *we*…see the need to be *benevolent,* I mean." The Cetin Man said.

"How is there a Cetin man in *my* citadel? I might imprison anyone who fails to give me a pleasing response." Emperor Colubrifer said.

"I see you brought an audience – they shall serve to test our new weapon." The Cetin Man said.

"There is no way that is a good thing for anyone but *them*." Caelifer said.

"Opinions are even divided about whether *violence in general* is *ever* a good thing." Arundineus said.

"*Whose* opinions?" Emperor Colubrifer said.

The Cetin Man closed his eyes and concentrated. Suddenly, Legionaire appeared, hovering near the Cetin Man.

"Look! Legionaire!" Caelifer said.

"I was meant to know *that* was the legionnaire you were looking for?!" Emperor Colubrifer said.

"Are the Cetin controlling him…but *how*?" Arundineus said.

"Restless Centurion!" The Cetin Man said.

A flaming red aura appeared around Legionaire.

"Attack the ones at the back first and kill anyone who stands between *you* and the enemy. My people want the Emperor to be powerless to stop his men being killed in front of him." The Cetin Man said.

Legionaire flew towards the group of legionnaires. He landed at the back of the group and started attacking nearby legionnaires. Legionnaires in the back of the group engaged Legionaire, but he killed several in short succession each with a single strike of his sword.

"Restless Centurion...I wonder." Caelifer said barely louder than a whisper.

"A ghost cannot kill the living...*can* it?" Emperor Colubrifer said.

"I am not sure I fully understand *what* Legionaire is." Arundineus said.

Legionaire reached the second row of legionnaires from the back. Again, legionnaires rushed at Legionaire and again were easily killed by him. Legionaire approached the middle row of legionnaires, who were much more hesitant to attack than the ones Legionaire had already killed.

"Something that Cetin man said – 'restless centurion'. I have a theory." Caelifer said.

"I have hardly ever known Caelifer to *not* have a theory." Arundineus said.

"I will indulge your theory only when we have no other options." Emperor Colubrifer said.

"I forgot how effective *your* plans to stop Legionaire were." Caelifer said.

"Think carefully about insulting an Emperor, I might *forget* to be merciful." Emperor Colubrifer said.

"'Restless Centurion' – it is rather simple – he should be vulnerable to magic that causes sleep." Caelifer said.

"Men, do any of you know sleep magic?" Emperor Colubrifer said.

"*I* know several basic elemental spells." A legionnaire at the front of the group said.

"I have mastered some basic restorative magic." Another legionnaire said.

"You never know when *defensive* magic might come in handy." A third legionnaire said.

"Probably when the *noble* Emperor realises none of you have the magic he *wants*, I would wager." Caelifer thought.

"Anyone else know magic? *Any* magic at all?" Emperor Colubrifer said.

The remaining legionnaires in the front row shook their heads in unison. Legionaire killed the middle row of legionnaires, but not as quickly as the previous two rows.

"If none of you knew sleep magic, you should have just *answered my question* in the first place." Emperor Colubrifer said.

"Talk about Emperor *Snake-mouthed*!" Caelifer thought.

"Actually, *I* know sleep magic. In fact, it is the *only* magic I ever learned." Caelifer said.

"If that raging Legionaire *is* actually vulnerable to sleep magic, put it to sleep and my men will take care of the rest." Emperor Colubrifer said.

"What prison is going to hold *Legionaire*?" Arundineus said.

"I trust his restlessness is *temporary*." Emperor Colubrifer said.

Legionaire approached the second row from the front of legionnaires.

"My men barely even seem to slow him down." Emperor Colubrifer said.

"Legionaire is some kind of 'warrior spirit'. Your men are not even fighting flesh and blood." Arundineus said.

"Flesh and blood can die...whatever Legionaire is *cannot*. I see your predicament." Caelifer said.

"*Do* you, though?" Emperor Colubrifer said.

Legionaire defeated the second row from the front of legionnaires, except for two who were only wounded rather than killed.

"Is that *mercy* I see?" Emperor Colubrifer said.

"What do *you* know about mercy?" Caelifer thought.

"Where are *my* ghost warriors?" Emperor Colubrifer said.

"Who said it was that simple?" Arundineus said.

Legionaire approached the front of the group of legionnaires. The last row of legionnaires fled rather than face the same fate as their fellow legionnaires.

"The gods will remember your cowardice!" Emperor Colubrifer said.

"And you think *you* are brave? The gods will let *anyone* think themselves brave these days." Caelifer thought.

Legionaire walked slowly towards Arundineus, Caelifer and Emperor Colubrifer.

"Defender of the Legion!" Arundineus said.

There was no reaction from Legionaire.

"Shield of the Legion!" Arundineus said.

Again, Legionaire was reactionless.

"What was *that* supposed to achieve?" Caelifer said.

"It might have freed him from mind control. It was worth a *try*, was it not?" Arundineus said.

Arundineus unsheathed his sword and assumed a defensive stance. Legionaire appeared to stare at Arundineus, as though recognising him, then looked at Caelifer and the Emperor.

"Kill those three and later you will take the capital together with my people!" The Cetin Man said.

"Why is *he* still here?" Arundineus said.

"Kill that Cetin monster already!" Emperor Colubrifer said.

"And defeat Legionaire at the same time? How do you expect us to do *that*?" Caelifer said.

"What was your name...Caelifer? Prepare the sleep magic." Emperor Colubrifer said.

"Will I be world-renowned for my ability to treat insomnia if this is successful?" Caelifer said.

"Renowned in the parts of the world not inhabited by the *Cetin*, at least." Emperor Colubrifer said.

Caelifer concentrated. A magic spell surrounded Legionaire. At first, Legionaire appeared unaffected, but then he stuck his sword in the ground for balance. The red aura surrounding him vanished.

"Whatever-it-was Vulgatus – can you and Caelifer handle that Cetin fool who should have fled when he had the chance?" Emperor Colubrifer asked.

"Hopefully?" Arundineus answered.

"I need to stay here to keep Legionaire from becoming restless." Caelifer said.

"I *might* be able to handle that 'Cetin fool', but he has a *name*, Emperor." Arundineus said.

"Which is?" Emperor Colubrifer said.

"How should *I* know?" Arundineus said.

"Then handle him, but find out his name before he stops breathing, would you?" Emperor Colubrifer said.

Arundineus pointed at the Cetin Man.

"Now is your last chance to flee, Cetin monster." Arundineus said.

"'Monster' is the most imaginative insult you could manage? I will not be fleeing from your insults, *that* much is certain." The Cetin Man said.

"If you will not *flee*, you will *die*!" Arundineus said.

Arundineus ran full speed towards the citadel while the Cetin Man looked on, seemingly with amusement. The doors of the citadel were unlocked, and Arundineus entered. There was a set of stairs in the distance leading to the balcony the Cetin Man was standing on.

"There are not many places to hide on a balcony!" Arundineus said.

Suddenly, the Cetin Man appeared near the base of the stairs and entered the lobby of the citadel.

"Say you take *my* life – one Cetin life lost, and, what was the number of legionnaires the Emperor lost today? *Some* might call that a successful battle." The Cetin Man said.

"If I wanted the opinions of those 'some', I would *ask* for them. You would sacrifice your *own* life for your people's ambitions?" Arundineus said.

"Surely you mean my people's *mad* ambitions?" The Cetin Man said.

"That is for the gods to judge…Deus Benevolus, if you are lucky. I assume you have a name?" Arundineus said.

"Icarus Megalo." Icarus Megalo said.

"From what I know of the Cetin, 'megalo' means 'great'. Hence, you are 'Icarus the Great'." Arundineus said.

"Rumours of my greatness may have been exaggerated." Icarus Megalo said.

"Which ones?" Arundineus said.

"Perhaps rumours *about* rumours of my greatness were what was exaggerated." Icarus Megalo said.

"Your *death* will be much more than a *rumour*." Arundineus said.

"Without Legionaire, your chances of killing me are less than assured." Icarus Megalo said.

"Even a *fair* chance of killing you is good enough for *me*." Arundineus said.

Arundineus assumed a defensive stance.

"You speak Verian almost flawlessly." Arundineus said.

"A means to an end, nothing more. Also, I believe *your* end is soon indeed." Icarus Megalo said.

Icarus Megalo summoned a spear of rock and threw it at Arundineus. It grazed his left shoulder.

"Do you still think your chance of killing me is 'fair'?" Icarus Megalo asked.

"Any chance better than *none* will work fine." Arundineus answered.

Arundineus raised his sword. Icarus Megalo summoned icicle daggers, which flew at Arundineus.

"Knowing basic elements, having fire magic would have been invaluable just now." Arundineus thought.

Arundineus blocked all but one of the icicle daggers – the one he failed to block struck him in the right of his torso.

"I make no apologies for my cold demeanour." Icarus Megalo said.

"What makes you think I would have *accepted* one?" Arundineus said.

Icarus Megalo cast a thunder spell, which sent a bolt of lightning directly towards Arundineus. Arundineus jumped to his left, and avoided the attack. Icarus Megalo cast a wind spell. Arundineus tightly grasped his sword with both hands and only barely prevented his sword being blown away.

"I take it you do not possess an inexhaustible supply of mana." Arundineus said.

"It will take more than defeating you to exhaust it, in any event." Icarus Megalo said.

"Do you think you have already won?" Arundineus said.

"Your chances are far worse than 'fair', it would seem. Your defeat is a *formality* at this point." Icarus Megalo said.

Suddenly, a red aura surrounded Arundineus. His eyes also turned scarlet.

"*This* cannot be good. Is this…" Icarus Megalo said.

Arundineus performed a flurry of six sword slashes.

Icarus Megalo dodged half of them, not all consecutively, but the other half of the sword slashes connected. Blood began gushing from Icarus Megalo's torso.

"My people would consider this…an *acceptable loss*." Icarus Megalo said.

"*My* loss would be unacceptable." Arundineus said.

Icarus Megalo died, and his body collapsed on the floor. The red aura surrounding Arundineus vanished and his eyes returned to their normal colour. Arundineus was breathing heavily.

"What in the gods' names just happened?" Arundineus said.

Shortly after, Arundineus re-joined the others.

"Burn Icarus Megalo's corpse before you do anything else." Arundineus said.

"A rather less ignominious name than I was expecting." Emperor Colubrifer said.

"Hopefully *you* suffer a rather *more* ignominious demise when you least expect it." Caelifer thought.

"Who is *Icarus Megalo*?" Caelifer asked.

"Never mind, he is *dead* now." Arundineus said.

No one else spoke.

"Is it safe to wake up Legionaire?" Arundineus said.

"If he starts becoming restless again, I know what to do." Caelifer said.

"Can you use magic to wake him up?" Arundineus asked.

"The strangest thing – when I learnt sleep magic, I did

not imagine I would be needing magic to *wake anyone up*." Caelifer answered.

"What kind of magician only learns a *single* magic spell?" Arundineus said.

"A *lazy* one, perhaps?" Caelifer said.

"Perhaps a tap from your sword, Vulgatus, will suffice?" Emperor Colubrifer said.

"He could hurt *you* far worse than you could ever hurt *him*." Caelifer said.

"I must have *really* needed that vote of confidence." Arundineus said.

Arundineus cautiously approached Legionaire and tapped Legionaire's left shoulder with his sword. Legionaire awakened almost immediately.

"Arundineus, Caelifer…and…why are you in the presence of the Verian Emperor?" Legionaire said.

"We never saw them coming." Arundineus said.

"Technically, we *did*, but we could not *stop* him coming." Caelifer thought.

"What do you mean?" Legionaire asked.

"You may want to look behind you." Arundineus said.

Legionaire turned and faced the bodies of the slaughtered legionnaires. He then turned back to Arundineus.

"What enemy has wrought such an atrocity?" Legionaire asked.

"How am I seeing and hearing a ghost?!" Emperor Colubrifer said.

"Why do I still have to see and hear *you*?" Caelifer thought.

"The Cetin attacked the capital." Arundineus said.

"And where was *I* during the incident?" Legionaire asked.

"He does not remember *anything* about that 'Restless Centurion' rampage?" Arundineus thought.

"That is unimportant. What is important is that the Cetin are now capable of attacking my precious capital, and I will not abide Cetin atrocities." Emperor Colubrifer said.

"Where are bodies from the Cetin who attacked? I see not a single Cetin corpse." Legionaire said.

Arundineus gulped.

"They…that is to say…" Arundineus said.

"We burned them. There was no chance we were going to offer our enemy the dignity of a proper burial." Emperor Colubrifer said.

"See to it that the men who so bravely defended the capital *are* given the dignity of a proper burial." Legionaire said.

"Am I to assume 'ghost' outranks 'Emperor'?" Emperor Colubrifer said.

"No disrespect was intended." Legionaire said.

"Which is more than can be said of Emperor Snake-mouthed." Caelifer thought.

"Wait. Why did you burn the Cetin corpses before burying your *own* men?" Legionaire said.

"Our hatred for the Cetin attackers got the better of us, that is all." Emperor Colubrifer said.

"Your hatred for the Cetin was *that* strong? Truly, you

are an emperor to be feared." Legionaire said.

"More like an emperor to be *forgotten*. Who would dare remember *you* fondly?" Caelifer thought.

"Legionaire, the Cetin covet your power. We must assume they will stop at nothing to obtain it." Arundineus said.

"I sensed the Cetin attempting to summon me earlier." Legionaire said.

"There is a place we may hide you, but it is not luxurious." Emperor Colubrifer said.

"Being *able* to hide me is in *itself* a luxury." Legionaire said.

"Yes, well, there is a catch. If you are awake, the enemy may attempt to control you." Emperor Colubrifer said.

"Must I be asleep to evade the enemy?" Legionaire asked.

"In a manner of speaking." Caelifer thought.

"Not permanently, only when there would be any danger of you encountering Cetin magicians capable of controlling you." Emperor Colubrifer said.

"Is there no other way?" Legionaire asked.

"Would not *you* know the answer to that better than *I* would?" Emperor Colubrifer answered.

"My being a spirit does not make me all-knowing." Legionaire said.

"Being all-knowing…is such a concept even *possible*, even if only for the gods?" Caelifer said.

"How can all knowledge be shared equally among all the gods? Surely that is not possible even for the gods." Emperor Colubrifer said.

"You might want to be careful how much you openly criticise the gods. Call it superstition, if you must." Legionaire said.

"Have you *met* any of the gods?" Emperor Colubrifer asked.

"One does not simply 'meet' a god." Legionaire said.

"Of course, discretion is a right of the gods." Emperor Colubrifer said.

"When do we make for your less-than-luxurious hiding place?" Legionaire asked.

"When would you *like* to make for the hiding place?" Emperor Colubrifer answered.

DEFY THY CAPTORS

Arundineus, Caelifer and Emperor Colubrifer were walking. There was a group of eighteen imperial soldiers accompanying Arundineus, Caelifer and Emperor Colubrifer. The group of the Emperor's soldiers was divided equally into legionnaires and archers. All of the legionnaires without exception were male, while about a third of the archers were female.

"Will not a group this size be easier for the Cetin to detect?" Arundineus asked.

"The larger the group, the greater the risk of spies." Emperor Colubrifer said.

"Anyone would think the Cetin have a nearly unlimited budget for spies the way *you* talk." Caelifer said.

"Do I detect a distinct hint of *insubordination*?" Emperor Colubrifer asked.

"Far more than a *hint*, Emperor Snake-tongue." Caelifer thought.

"Insubordination is intolerable." Emperor Colubrifer said.

"So are *you*. So is the thought you were actually *chosen* to be emperor." Caelifer thought.

"Empire is built upon *obedience*, not *rebellion*." Emperor Colubrifer said.

"Obedience or *slavery*? I doubt *you* know the difference." Caelifer thought.

"Exactly – *obedience*." Emperor Colubrifer said.

"I could not help but notice some of the archers are female." Arundineus said.

"Are you afraid a female lacks the strength to pull a bow string?" One of the female archers said.

"Surely we men *exaggerate* the inferiority of female strength?" Arundineus said.

"Surely you men exaggerate the *glory of battle* also." The same female archer said.

"Surely not?" Arundineus said.

One of the female archers glanced at another of them.

"He feels *threatened* by a woman capable of violence. Afraid of a woman who could hurt you *physically* as easily as *emotionally*, Arundineus?" The second female archer said.

"*Should* I be?" Arundineus asked.

"I doubt you could hurt *me* emotionally. My *emotions* are more resilient than my *muscles*." The second female archer said.

"A woman's heart might well be the most mysterious of her muscles." Arundineus said almost as quietly as a whisper.

"Are those two *serious* about each other or *not*?" Caelifer thought.

"I take it you are not an expert in *women's muscles*,

then?" The second female archer said.

"Careful, you might give the wrong kinds of people the wrong kind of ideas." The third female archer said.

Suddenly, a group of thirteen Cetin ambushed the Emperor's group. The Cetin group consisted of six swordsmen, six archers and what looked like a white-haired sorceress. A third of the Cetin group, including the sorceress, had yellow eyes, while the rest had red eyes.

"Only one of us here cannot be killed. A power worth killing for." The enemy sorceress said.

"Then do you volunteer to die for it?" Arundineus said.

"It is too early to predict who will survive." The enemy sorceress said.

"I will have all of your heads on pikes!" Emperor Colubrifer said.

"You will have the shame of defeat instead." The enemy sorceress said.

"Is this all the enemy could muster?" Arundineus said.

"Wait! The Cetin woman appears to be a magician!" Caelifer said.

"Why is Legionaire still awake? Stop acting the fool, Caelifer." Emperor Colubrifer said.

"It is *young* Caelifer to *you*." Caelifer said.

"It will be *dead* Caelifer if you do not hurry." Emperor Colubrifer said.

"Does your *mother* know what you do with your mouth?" Caelifer thought.

Legionaire glanced at the enemy sorceress.

"My power is not yours to abuse!" Legionaire said.

"Obeying willingly is simply a *formality*." The enemy sorceress said.

"Free will is *not* a *formality*!" Legionaire said.

"Kill the two guarding the emperor, you may capture the rest if you wish." The enemy sorceress said.

The Cetin group and the Emperor's soldiers engaged each other.

"You are not secretly versed in strong magic, are you, Emperor?" Caelifer asked.

"Attack these Cetin and risk exposing my secret, un-equalled magic ability?" Emperor Colubrifer answered.

"In these circumstances, *yes*." Caelifer said.

"Do you not realise I was *joking*?" Emperor Colubrifer said.

The Cetin group displayed surprising combat prowess given their numerical disadvantage. Two of the Emperor's swordsmen and two of the Emperor's male archers were dispatched without a single Cetin casualty.

"Clearly *these* enemies have seen battle before." Emperor Colubrifer said.

"Could you have stated anything *more* obvious?" Caelifer thought.

Caelifer cast the same spell he used to put Legionaire to sleep in the capital. The enemy sorceress clenched one of her hands and a flaming whip shot towards Caelifer. At the last moment, Caelifer ducked, and the whip narrowly missed the top of his head.

"Legionaire will not respond to anything you say unless he wakes up. If you had focused all your manpower on killing *me*, you might have had a chance." Caelifer said.

"Is sleep magic the only trick you know? What good will that do you against a sorceress?" The enemy sorceress said.

"If you plan to kill us, can you at least tell us your name?" Arundineus said.

"Selene. The only other time you will need to know my name is in the next world if anyone asks how you died. You will remember to tell them Sorceress Selene sent you, will you not?" Selene said.

"The sorceress is the *true* threat! Whoever manages to spill her filthy Cetin blood will receive a year's wages." Emperor Colubrifer said.

"If anyone was to spill your blood, I hope they do it for *free*." Caelifer thought.

The Emperor's soldiers fought more ardently. One of the Emperor's swordsmen achieved an unusually lucky dodge by some fluke and proceeded to finish off his opponent. However, one of the Cetin swordsmen connected a blow to his non-sword arm.

"If I die *here*, may the gods protect the emperor." The lucky swordsman said.

"I am rather skeptical about appeals for divine protection. The gods either have incurable apathy, are less powerful than we imagine, or perhaps might not even exist to begin with." Selene said.

"Deus Benevolus, protect me if you are not afflicted with

incurable apathy, or indeed, if you actually exist." Emperor Colubrifer said.

"Deus *Benevolus*? What god is *that*?" Selene said.

"Where are so many Cetin learning to speak almost flawless Verian? If there are language teachers I do not know about, I shall have to increase their taxes." Emperor Colubrifer said.

"A *book* could be filled with the things *you* do not know about. If the gods had a plan for *you*, they must be good at keeping secrets." Caelifer thought.

The Cetin group killed two more of the Emperor's male archers and two more of the Emperor's swordsmen, and suffered a single casualty in the process.

"Where are you going with Legionaire? Our spies only know there is a hiding place, not where it is." Selene said.

"If you kill Emperor Colubrifer, it will be all-out war between the Verian Empire and the Cetin – are you insane enough to *desire* that?" Arundineus said.

"*My* forces are winning, what have you to say to *that*?" Selene said.

"You have not witnessed the true measure of my strength." Arundineus said.

"I appreciate your confidence, young Arundineus, but the gods could not have chosen a worse time for bravado." Emperor Colubrifer said.

"I will witness either the true measure of your strength, or your death. Either will prove satisfying." Selene said.

Selene ran towards Arundineus. She cast a wind spell,

which knocked him onto his back on the ground.

"Our spies would have informed us if you actually possessed any undesirable power." Selene said.

"A human with *any* power would be *your* definition of 'undesirable power.'" Arundineus said.

"If you will not display your mythical, hidden 'true' strength, you will *die*. You *must* die." Selene said.

Selene cast an earth spell, which turned the ground beneath Arundineus into a clay-like consistency, hindering his movement. Arundineus attempted to attack Selene with his sword, but his hindered movements were too slow to catch Selene off-guard.

"How many others can control Legionaire?" Selene asked.

"I should be asking *you* that question." Arundineus answered.

"How many other *humans* can control Legionaire?" Selene asked.

"Tell her *nothing*, Arundineus, or I will make sure *nothing* is what remains of your legacy." Emperor Colubrifer said.

"What makes you think *your* legacy is so impressive?" Caelifer thought.

Selene cast a thunder spell, which summoned a ball of lightning in her left hand. She threw it at Arundineus, but as it connected, it re-awakened the mysterious power he used against Icarus Megalo, and his eyes turned scarlet again and he became surrounded by a red aura once again.

Arundineus leapt to his feet, and swung his sword. Selene dodged, then dodged a second swing, before she then summoned a magical barrier to withstand the third swing.

"Where have you *acquired* this power?" Selene asked.

"The gods, maybe. I cannot say for sure. But I *can* say for sure that if *this* is the best you can manage, *you* will die." Arundineus answered.

"*Kill* the demon witch, and do it quickly!" Emperor Colubrifer said.

"A great role model for *morality*, you certainly are *not*." Caelifer thought.

"My magical barrier still holds. Did you overestimate your strength?" Selene said.

"I underestimated the strength of your *barrier*, nothing more." Arundineus said.

Arundineus slashed three times consecutively. Selene's barrier withstood the first two slashes, then appeared to weaken considerably when the third slash connected.

"How is that demon witch not *dead* yet?" Emperor Colubrifer said.

"How are *you* still in power?" Caelifer thought.

Suddenly, Arundineus's mysterious power faded before he could land any decisive blows against Selene.

Selene scoffed.

"I was worried about a mysterious, yet apparently *unreliable* power. Was I the *fool* for being worried, or were *you* the fool for blindly believing in that power?" Selene said.

"We *both* are fools." Arundineus said.

"*They* admit to being fools but Emperor Snake-handler does *not*? Is there any *justice* in this world?!" Caelifer thought.

Suddenly, the remaining archers loyal to the Emperor concentrated their fire on Selene. The first arrow was stopped by her magical barrier, the second arrow dispelled her magical barrier, then the rest of the arrows struck Selene. Meanwhile, the remaining Cetin archers attacked whichever targets they deemed fit in the opening the remaining Imperial archers had created. Selene fell to one knee.

"My people will have your *heads* for this insult." Selene said.

"This is why some people detest violence. Violence leads to more violence. *Our* people are no better than *yours* in that regard." Arundineus said.

"*Our* people no better than the *Cetin*? Surely a touch of dark humour?" Emperor Colubrifer said.

"My people do not *fear* violence. No, we would fear… unattainable peace being….forever unattainable." Selene said.

Selene died and her arrow-filled body fell to the ground. Most of the remaining Imperial archers besides the three female archers were felled by the Cetin archers. The Cetin forces now had a slight numerical advantage.

"If we awaken Legionaire, these remaining foes will be defeated in the blink of an eye." Emperor Colubrifer said.

"There might be some other enemy magician lurking nearby." Caelifer said.

"One with the greatest magic trick of all – *invisibility*." Arundineus said.

"Of course! There was some other magician who turned invisible to catch us off-guard." Caelifer said.

"Why do people sometimes fail to recognise *humour*?" Arundineus said.

"The lady Selene has fallen. We should have been *assured* victory with that Animus asleep." One of the Cetin swordsmen said.

"Even if we kill the man who has sleep magic, without a magician, we are finished if that Animus awakens." Another Cetin swordsman said.

"Having a numerical advantage is not *good enough* for you Cetin scum?" Emperor Colubrifer said.

"We have yet to kill either of the two Selene ordered us to kill, and the Verian Emperor is too well defended. Perhaps we should retreat." The first Cetin swordsman said.

"You did not so much as learn the location of our hiding place for Legionaire. This little skirmish has availed you *nothing*." Emperor Colubrifer said.

"*Availed nothing* – much like some of your *leadership*." Caelifer thought.

"How could their spies know there was a *secret hiding place* for Legionaire but *not* know how many soldiers the Emperor was travelling with?" Arundineus said.

"How could they be so confident of winning with fewer numbers? Battles being won with fewer numbers is what they *write poems about*. In case it was not obvious, there are *not many* of those poems." Caelifer said.

"We needed more information about the Emperor's movements..." The first Cetin swordsman said.

"You mean his *travelling arrangements*. The Emperor's *bowels* are of no interest to us, unless regarding a plan to *remove* them." The second Cetin swordsman said.

"We would be doomed as soon that Animus awakens. If we flee *now*, at least we escape with our *lives*." The first Cetin swordsman said.

"Does anyone *object* to retreating?" The second Cetin swordsman said.

All of the remaining Cetin soldiers retreated.

"Are you not going to tell them the gods will remember their cowardice, or some such?" Caelifer said.

"There will be *poems* and *plays* written about the Cetin cowards who had a numerical advantage yet fled!" Emperor Colubrifer shouted.

"Incidentally, where *is* the supposed hiding place?" Arundineus asked.

"*Actual, not supposed*, and you will *know* soon enough." Emperor Colubrifer answered.

"Shall I wake up Legionaire?" Caelifer asked.

"Very well. I see no signs of an enemy magician." Emperor Colubrifer answered.

Some indeterminate amount of time later, the group arrived at the entrance to a cave.

"The hiding place is a *cave*?" Arundineus said.

"You will refer to this location as Hidden Mystery."

Emperor Colubrifer said.

"Could the name *be* any more mysterious?" Caelifer asked.

"If it *can*, then the name of this location will need to be even *more* cryptic." Emperor Colubrifer said.

"Figuring *you* out is not cryptic *enough*?" Caelifer thought.

"I understand that with a hiding place like *this*, you can keep the entrance well-guarded, but how can any of your forces inside escape to safety in an *emergency*?" Arundineus asked.

"If only we had a magician *capable* of making something invisible." Emperor Colubrifer answered.

"If we *did*, they should start with *you*. Then, we would simply need *another* magician capable of making noises *silent*, and then we can count ourselves lucky." Caelifer thought.

"Have you not considered the possibility there might still be a spy nearby?" Arundineus asked.

"Would it not be the greatest of ironies if the *Emperor* was secretly a spy? Imagine *that* – I do not want to." Caelifer thought.

"The *gods* know where the hiding place is – do you think they can be trusted to not tell the *Cetin*?" Caelifer said.

"*Our* gods would not be the problem; it would be *their* gods." Emperor Colubrifer said.

"Is talking to the gods something you can find a *magician* for?" Caelifer said.

"Why *not*? It seems you can find a magician for almost everything *else*." Emperor Colubrifer said.

"It *does* seem like that, does it not?" Caelifer said.

"I cannot be certain none of you are spies, but please, come explore Hidden Mystery." Emperor Colubrifer said.

"The Emperor saying the word 'please'...maybe he *has* learned some kind of magic." Caelifer thought.

Later that day, the group was deep inside the cave. Legionaire was present and awake, and surrounded by most of the group except for the female archers who were guarding the entrance and therefore absent from the group.

"If the Cetin launched a determined attack, we only have *three* archers guarding the entrance." Arundineus said.

"Then you must trust those three women were chosen for their skill, not their physical strength." Emperor Colubrifer said.

"When you woke me after that battle, I asked you why you burned those Cetin bodies in Magna Gloria so quickly but had not already burned the bodies of the Cetin you fought before we reached this cave. I thought about the response you gave me – were you being *honest*?" Legionaire said.

"Does he suspect we have not told the *truth* about what happened in the capital?" Arundineus thought.

"When we entered the capital...I felt an unusual sensation, then remember nothing between then and when we were near that citadel." Legionaire said.

"What can we tell him without telling the truth? We

could use the gods' help now." Arundineus thought.

"Did something happen in the capital?" Legionaire asked.

"Something *definitely* happened in the capital." Caelifer thought.

"The important thing is that the Cetin do not gain control of your power." Arundineus said.

"I killed that spy in the forest – should I have not neglected to also kill his messenger bird?" Legionaire asked.

"*Probably.*" Caelifer thought.

"If we made a mistake by not killing the messenger bird, the gods will make sure we *learn* from that mistake." Arundineus said.

"As a rule, we should remain vigilant to reduce the ability of Cetin spies to create problems for us." Legionaire said.

"Cetin spies seem to make it their *goal in life* to create problems for us." Caelifer said.

"Their spies would appear to be more *numerous* than we expected." Emperor Colubrifer said.

"That is one of the most sensible things I have actually heard you *say*." Caelifer thought.

"Do you expect us to sleep on a rough cave floor?" Arundineus asked.

"You *will* if you want to avoid being arrested for disobedience." Emperor Colubrifer said.

"*His* definition of disobedience is definitely *not* sensible." Caelifer thought.

"If anyone *else* objects to sleeping here, you can sleep

outside the cave, but know you will forfeit your wages."
Emperor Colubrifer said.

Some of the soldiers grumbled. That night, Arundineus
dreamed. An image of Icarus Megalo's face appeared in his
mind.

"What was that strange power I defeated him with?
Where did he learn to speak Verian so well? Did he have
children that were left fatherless when I killed him?"
Arundineus thought.

Icarus Megalo's face disappeared from Arundineus's
mind and Selene's face then appeared in his mind.

"She would have stopped at nothing to control Legionaire. How did the Cetin learn to control Legionaire? Was
there a traitor who taught them? Questions, yet so few
answers." Arundineus thought.

Selene's face disappeared from Arundineus's mind.

"Do the Cetin consider the *Verian Empire* evil? Do they
consider *humans* evil? What if their definitions of good
and evil are nothing like we thought? *We* could be committing evil for no reason. The Cetin might not *fear* violence,
but surely not even the Cetin want *never-ending* violence.
Perhaps we know less about them than we thought."
Arundineus thought.

Emperor Colubrifer's face appeared in Arundineus's
mind.

"Was he really the best leader the Verian Empire could
offer? But what alternatives do we *have*? He is still prefer-
able to *anarchy* – the Empire would not *survive* anarchy.

Leadership demands responsibility. It cannot be easy being burdened with the responsibilities of leadership. What person with sanity would *want* that?" Arundineus thought.

Emperor Colubrifer's face disappeared from Arundineus's mind and the face of the second female archer appeared in Arundineus's mind.

"Why would *her* face appear? Does this mean I have feelings for her? But I do not even know her *name*…is it actually possible to love someone you do not know? If she does not have any feelings for *me*, it would be a doomed romance that *ended* before it *began*. Why would I have feelings for her? What reasons could there be?" Arundineus thought.

The second female archer's face disappeared from Arundineus's mind and Caelifer's face appeared.

"Caelifer, a true friend. Without *you*, Legionaire would have killed us and the Emperor. Thank the gods you took magic seriously enough even if to only have learned sleep magic. We were lucky to have you." Arundineus thought.

The following morning, Arundineus awoke to find the rest of the group except the three female archers already awake. The Emperor appeared irritated.

"If your dreams are *that* exciting, you could be thrown into a prison cell where you will have all the time you *want* to dream." Emperor Colubrifer said.

"The Verian Empire needs to dream of *better leadership*." Caelifer thought.

"If dreams are from the gods, how would they feel if you

had made dreaming a crime? Would you dare offend the gods?" Arundineus asked.

"Probably even our *bowel movements* offend the gods. How can one ever be sure they are *not* offending the gods?" Emperor Colubrifer said.

"There is far too much talk of *bowel movements* lately. Can we make a movement *away* from that subject?" Caelifer said.

"Movement towards *what* topic, exactly?" Emperor Colubrifer asked.

"Any topic not involving *bodily functions*, if I may make a suggestion." Arundineus answered.

"Arundineus, Caelifer, you are to return with me to Magna Gloria soon, now that Hidden Mystery is secure." Emperor Colubrifer said.

"If the gods *are* offended by our bowel movements, why would they create us with that *necessity*?" Arundineus asked.

"You are talking about the *gods* – why should it have to make sense to *you*?" Caelifer answered.

"Perhaps the gods needed something to *pity* us for." Emperor Colubrifer said.

"By *your* logic, the gods created us simply so they could pity us. Is your theory that pity is some kind of *nectar* to the gods?" Caelifer said.

"Some might consider *wine* a nectar of the gods." Emperor Colubrifer said.

"The nectar of *Bacchus*, at least." Caelifer said.

"Arundineus, Caelifer, when I am ready to leave, I expect

to embark *promptly*. Legionaire will remain within Hidden Mystery for as long as possible." Emperor Colubrifer said.

"What you *expect* and what you will *get* are *two different things*." Caelifer thought.

GROWING TENSIONS

Arundineus, Caelifer, and Emperor Colubrifer arrived in Magna Gloria on horseback. They stopped their horses and dismounted. Two men nearby approached, grabbed the reins, and led the horses away.

"I will give a speech near the citadel in short order. I have a fitting plan to honour those who the Cetin forced Legionaire to kill against his will." Emperor Colubrifer said.

"A fitting plan? *Your* plans are not what I would call 'fitting'. Well, plans fitting the definition of *terrible*, perhaps." Caelifer thought.

"I am sure I have no idea what the phrase 'a fitting plan' means." Arundineus said.

"Nor *need* you know…*yet*." Emperor Colubrifer said.

"How soon will the speech be?" Arundineus asked.

"Tonight, enjoy not having to sleep on a rough surface, and there might be news tomorrow regarding when the speech will occur. A room is booked at an inn for you both, tonight only. Free of charge, of course." Emperor Colubrifer answered.

"I almost feel *sorry* for the *inn-keeping* profession." Caelifer said.

"It would be shameful for two heroes of the Empire to be exploited by profit-obsessed inn-keepers." Emperor Colubrifer said.

"Inn-keepers are probably an honourable profession. A profit-obsessed *brothel* owner I *would* be concerned about." Caelifer said.

"I shall have to have inns inspected to make sure they are not secretly a brothel." Emperor Colubrifer said.

"Emperor Colubrifer, ridding the world of concealed brothels. A champion of justice *you* are." Caelifer thought.

"Assuming the inn you booked is respectable, we appreciate your generosity." Arundineus said.

"One night at an inn for two people, he is the *definition* of charitable, is he not?" Caelifer thought.

"I shall have a man lead you to the inn in question." Emperor Colubrifer said.

"Thank you. That was thoughtful of you." Arundineus said.

"His thoughts are his biggest problems – specifically, his *negative* thoughts." Caelifer thought.

"I hope you are well-rested when I make my speech. Somnus guide your dreams tonight." Emperor Colubrifer said.

"That one actually *was* thoughtful." Caelifer thought.

Later that night, Arundineus and Caelifer were at an inn, in the same room, with separate beds.

"Pity I could not have spent tonight in the company of a fine woman." Arundineus said.

"Did you have one in mind? Wait. Is there someone you are developing *feelings* for?" Caelifer asked.

"I do not know…there *might* be someone, but I do not even know her name." Arundineus answered.

"Are you falling for that female archer?" Caelifer asked.

"What? Why do you say *that*?" Arundineus answered.

"You and her might have a future. Do you consider her attractive?" Caelifer said.

"Why are we even *talking* about this? If *she* has no feelings for *me*, our budding romance would be cut short before it even had a *chance* to bloom." Arundineus said.

"Talk to her, and you will know for sure." Caelifer said.

"If I do not even know her name, where am I supposed to *meet* her? *How* would I be supposed to meet her?" Arundineus said.

"My expertise on love is not much greater than *yours*. If there is a way to her heart, you will *find* it." Caelifer said.

"I would have to find *her* first before trying to find a way to her *heart*." Arundineus said.

"Just make sure your feelings for her are not entirely based on her…*physical* aspects." Caelifer said.

"How will I know if is truly love and not simply lust?" Arundineus asked.

"I did not say anything about *lust*. Did you think it was *implied*?" Caelifer answered.

"What else is 'physical aspects' supposed to mean?" Arundineus asked.

"Even some *lovers* might not be sure if it is love or lust.

Stop worrying so much." Caelifer answered.

"'Stop worrying so much'? Is that the best you could come up with?" Arundineus said.

"Would you prefer if I said 'worry like there is no tomorrow and do not listen to anything I say'?" Caelifer said.

"'Like there is no tomorrow'? Whoever came up with such a *gloomy* sentiment?" Arundineus asked.

"Someone far more gloomy than either of *us*, I suspect." Caelifer answered.

"The only way that sentiment could be true is for a person who *dies* today. I do not want to talk about who will be *dying* today, not even if *I* was the one dying." Arundineus said.

"'Like there is no tomorrow' is only a figure of speech, not even one I like *using*, at that." Caelifer said.

"Perhaps Deus Benevolus might approve of romantic intentions." Arundineus said.

"If he *exists*. You would think a benevolent god would do more to *make his existence known*." Caelifer said.

"What will the Emperor's speech be about?" Arundineus asked.

Caelifer yawned then fell asleep.

"Maybe Deus Benevolus helped you to fall asleep just now. Even if Deus Benevolus is a *myth*, it is a *comforting* myth." Arundineus thought.

The next day, Caelifer and Arundineus approached the area near the citadel – the area where Legionaire had

rampaged under the control of the Cetin. There was a large crowd. Arundineus and Caelifer approached the crowd.

"Do you think the Emperor *paid* these people to attend his speech? Knowing *him*, I would not want to do *anything* for him for *free*." Caelifer said.

"Except *hold a low opinion of him*." Arundineus said.

"Something like that." Caelifer said.

The second female archer approached.

"You are that archer...I did not expect to see you here."

"Is that your idea of *romantic*?" Caelifer thought.

"I *am* 'that archer', and 'that archer' happens to be named Pugna Prudentia." Pugna said.

"Pugna...a strong name for a strong woman." Arundineus said.

"Strong, you say? I think I will go ahead and gladly accept the compliment." Pugna said.

"What could the Emperor be planning?" Arundineus asked.

"Your romance skills are starting to *fail*." Caelifer thought.

"Unless the Emperor is planning to *become a decent person*, I could hardly care *less* what he is planning." Pugna said.

"Sounds like something *I* might have come up with." Caelifer thought.

"Are you staying long in Magna Gloria?" Arundineus asked.

"Very long – I happen to *live* here in the capital. What about *you*?" Pugna answered.

"I hail from a mostly insignificant town called Parvulus." Arundineus said.

"Were there no *attractive women* in Parvulus, or even worse, were there no women *at all* there?" Pugna asked.

"What is *this*? You might have got her *attention*, friend." Caelifer thought.

"Matters of the heart are rather mysterious." Arundineus said.

"I suspect they *are*. How does a town manage to be *mostly* insignificant? Are not towns generally either significant *or* insignificant?" Pugna said.

"Does she want to know more *about* you?" Caelifer thought.

"Parvulus was where Legionaire was first summoned. Well, maybe not *first* summoned – the magicians seemed to have already *heard* of Legionaire. You would think if Legionaire had been summoned in the past, there would have at least been a *book* mentioning it." Arundineus said.

"Perhaps someday you will need to show me around Parvulus." Pugna said.

"It looks like the two of you have *potential*." Caelifer thought.

"How far away is your house from here?" Arundineus asked.

"I will tell you *later...privately*." Pugna answered.

"You might *like* where this is going." Caelifer thought.

"A private conversation with Pugna? Is this the beginning of a budding romance?" Arundineus thought.

Emperor Colubrifer emerged from the ground floor of the citadel and began approaching the area in front of the crowd.

"Feel free to disagree, his name is Emperor Snake-haired, but does he not seem more like Emperor Snake-*tongue*?" Caelifer asked.

Arundineus and Pugna both laughed.

"How long have you been *waiting* to make that joke?" Arundineus asked.

"Who said I *waited*?" Caelifer answered.

"Speaking of *waiting*…" Arundineus said.

Emperor Colubrifer reached the centre of the area in front of the crowd and stopped.

"Loyal citizens of the esteemed Verian Empire, I, Emperor Cincinnatus Colubrifer have granted you all an audience today." Emperor Colubrifer said.

"More like we granted *him* an audience." Caelifer said.

"At least he called us 'loyal citizens' and not *peasants*." Arundineus said.

"The Verian Empire is under threat from the detested Cetin. We cannot allow transgressions to go unpunished." Emperor Colubrifer said.

"*Your* transgressions go *unpunished* all the time." Caelifer thought.

"Is he planning *revenge*? An *esteemed Empire* that is not above revenge?" Pugna said.

"It would be a tragedy for us to desire war *more* than the Cetin." Arundineus said.

"The Cetin would seek to exploit *any* weakness they can find in the Empire. We cannot fight them with *weakness*, only with *strength*." Emperor Colubrifer said.

"Have you noticed how much of his speech consists of the words 'we cannot'? Apparently, *we could not* find someone to *write a better speech*." Caelifer said.

"Maybe Deus Benevolus *should* have found someone." Arundineus said.

"Is Deus Benevolus a *title* for a god, a *new* god, or some king of the gods we never heard of?" Caelifer said.

"Hopefully Deus Benevolus *is* a king of the gods we never heard of – we would *need* a benevolent god considering the kind of business the god *Mars* is associated with. Unless Deus Benevolus is what you would get if Mars fell *deeply in love* with Venus." Pugna said.

"Hostilities between the Empire and the Cetin are increasing and if we do not respond to Cetin aggression, war might eventually be inevitable regardless of how ardent our diplomacy may be." Emperor Colubrifer said.

"Ardent diplomacy – something I doubt you are even *capable* of." Caelifer thought.

"Hurry up and announce war against the Cetin! You nearly have *already*." Arundineus said.

"If there is a *spy* in the crowd, they are going to want to charge a *fortune* for information about this speech. I am not contemplating a change of career just yet, though." Caelifer said.

"Cetin aggression recently occurred in Magna Gloria in

this very area. A minor attack in Magna Gloria could easily become a series of skirmishes, and a series of skirmishes risks war. Do you want your children to tell *their* children of the atrocities of the Cetin, forever poisoning their *perception* of the Cetin?" Emperor Colubrifer said.

"You *already* seem to be afflicted by poisoned perceptions, and I doubt your parents were telling you *bedtime stories* about Cetin atrocities." Caelifer thought.

"Even if the Cetin committed atrocities, if he has *us* commit atrocities to punish them for *their* atrocities, that does not make us *better* than them." Pugna said.

"A strong woman with strong opinions." Arundineus thought.

"Deus Benevolus make that Emperor see reason!" Arundineus said.

"Why did we wait until *now* to make a prayer like that?" Caelifer said.

"*You* might have more of an idea than *I* do." Arundineus said.

"If only Deus Benevolus could make problems disappear with a simple prayer." Pugna said.

"We cannot be certain Deus Benevolus could make problems disappear even with a *complex* prayer." Caelifer said.

"To give the Cetin pause, I declare my intent to have as many Cetin either captured or killed as possible. We will not stop until they beg us for mercy, perhaps not *even* then." Emperor Colubrifer said.

"The Cetin begging for mercy would not be *enough* for you? When have the *Cetin* ever begged for mercy?" Caelifer thought.

"But what about Cetin traders who *rely* on trade with the Verian Empire? Will being Cetin alone make them guilty of a crime even if they are innocent of any crimes?" Pugna asked.

"Cetin traders would make terrible spies anyway. Green skin makes it *very* obvious they are not *human*." Arundineus answered.

"Would he order even Cetin *infants* to be captured or killed? Emperor Colubrifer, the baby-stealer, or *even*, Emperor Colubrifer, the baby-*killer*." Caelifer thought.

"How can the Verian Empire *go* down this path?" Pugna asked.

"*Too easily*, it would seem. To think I was almost starting to grow *fond* of Emperor Snake-bite." Caelifer said.

"Is the *Emperor* the biting snake, or are *you*?" Arundineus thought.

"A snake-bite would almost be too *good* for him." Pugna said.

"The punishment for those found guilty of being a spy will henceforth be much greater. Any spies unwilling to reveal information about the enemy will be executed if caught." Emperor Colubrifer said.

"Maybe snake-bites will be used as a form of punishment. History will never forget the *Snake Emperor*. History might *want* to forget him, though." Caelifer said.

"What *he* is proposing is *tyranny*." Arundineus said.

"I would say 'there is a first time for everything'…if tyranny was actually a *foreign concept* to the Verian Empire." Caelifer said.

A man near the front of the crowd, close to Emperor Colubrifer, brandished a dagger.

"Today tyranny dies!" The man who brandished the dagger shouted.

The man rushed towards Emperor Colubrifer. Several imperial soldiers who were holding back the crowd advanced on the man.

"Today *traitors* die." One of the imperial soldiers said.

The man attacked the imperial soldiers wildly, but after a brief struggle, was stabbed multiple times, once by each of the imperial soldiers present. The dagger-wielding man collapsed and his body was lifeless.

"That man deserved an *army*." Caelifer said.

"In death, he might still *get* one." Arundineus said.

"I seem to have temporarily lost my composure after that…act of insolence. I will not *abide* treason." Emperor Colubrifer said.

"What *difference* does it make? You do not even abide *acting like a decent person*." Caelifer thought.

"Treason is utterly unacceptable. Are there any *other* traitors among you?" Emperor Colubrifer said.

No one in the crowd left their position.

"Anyone caught aiding enemy spies will risk execution unless Deus Benevolus somehow moves me to mercy."

Emperor Colubrifer said.

"Now comes a lengthy list of things *now* considered *crimes*. Wait for it." Caelifer said.

"New laws shall be devised to weaken Cetin influence." Emperor Colubrifer said.

"How did you *know*?" Pugna asked.

"How did you *not* know?" Caelifer answered.

"Rest assured, the Cetin will not find us to be weak." Emperor Colubrifer said.

"No, but your sense of *morals* will be found to be weak." Caelifer thought.

"What insanity will befall the Empire *now*?" Pugna asked.

"Insanity is a good choice of word." Arundineus answered.

"We shall see how *esteemed* our Empire is once insanity has *truly set in*." Caelifer said.

"Are the *Cetin* either this insane or more so?" Arundineus asked.

"Probably not *more so*." Caelifer answered.

"How *reassuring*." Arundineus said.

"We will not be defeated by the Cetin. We will not let them gain the advantage. We will not deign to give them mercy while they offer atrocities in response." Emperor Colubrifer said.

"So he has gone from 'we *cannot*' to 'we *will* not'? How *innovative*." Caelifer said.

"We will root out treachery wherever it may be found."

Emperor Colubrifer said.

"Is he *still* going with the 'we will' statements?" Caelifer said.

"Apparently so." Arundineus said.

"The Cetin will find few points of weakness in our resolve, but they may find points of weakness in their *own* resolve." Emperor Colubrifer said.

"So now he wants to take every opportunity to insult the Cetin? This speech is failing to *move me*." Caelifer said.

"Look around – *some* people are being *moved* by it." Arundineus said.

"Does he want us to fight the Cetin by behaving *worse* than them?" Pugna asked.

"If you hear of a speech like this in *Cetin* territories, I will pay you a month's wages." Caelifer answered.

"Have I neglected anything?" Emperor Colubrifer said.

"You definitely *have* – not least of all, *remembering to be a good person*." Caelifer said.

Emperor Colubrifer appeared to ponder, his expression that of being puzzled.

"If someone actually *wrote* that speech, they seemed rather fond of *repetition*." Caelifer said.

"Maybe they wanted the message to be *clear*." Pugna said.

"The message is definitely *clear* – tyranny is *back* and making up for lost time." Caelifer said.

"Be vigilant and report suspected spies immediately. Those found to be complicit with enemy spies will be imprisoned unless their involvement is great enough to warrant immediate execution." Emperor Colubrifer said.

"You would think spies were everywhere including *inside chamber pots* listening to *him* talk." Caelifer said.

"I hope Somnus gives our *glorious Emperor* bad dreams tonight." Arundineus said.

"Only *tonight*?" Caelifer said.

"Surely you mean *especially* tonight." Pugna said.

"How much longer is he going to *continue* this *public display of madness*?" Caelifer asked.

"Serve your Empire without hesitation, and your lives will be comfortable. Betray the Empire and you can be assured your lives will difficult, as difficult as a traitor deserves. Return now to your homes or places of work and know that loyalty will be rewarded and betrayal will be punished." Emperor Colubrifer said.

Emperor Colubrifer approached a nearby imperial soldier and whispered something to him. He then began approaching the ground floor of the citadel, followed by roughly a third of the imperial soldiers present at the speech, while the rest remained behind to hold back the crowd.

"You were *saying*?" Arundineus asked.

"The gods must have found a cure for their *apathy*." Caelifer answered.

"What made you think something like that was *impossible*?" Arundineus asked.

"So the gods' apathy *is* a treatable affliction!" Pugna answered.

"*Now* you might be starting to get *carried away*." Caelifer said.

"What *now*? Wait and see how *far* and how *quickly* the Verian Empire sinks into the depths of insanity?" Arundineus asked.

"'Depths' of insanity…I *like* that, rather *poetic*." Caelifer answered.

"I suppose we keep serving the Empire and keep our heads down." Arundineus said.

"We would *need* to if we wanted to keep out of prison, or for that matter, *keep on living*." Caelifer said.

"Tyranny or death…those are *not* good choices, *are* they?" Pugna asked.

"Maybe death has some kind of *appeal*, I do not know." Arundineus answered.

Emperor Colubrifer entered the citadel, followed by his security detail.

"Tyranny will be truly back and flourishing in *no time at all*." Caelifer said.

"How do you manage to see the *humour* in times like these?" Arundineus asked.

"I was *born* that way, I suppose." Caelifer answered.

"Jokes like *yours* will probably be *illegal* soon." Pugna said.

"It would certainly kill *some* people to actually *have* a sense of humour in the first place." Caelifer said.

"Pugna, did you say you live *here*, in the capital?" Arundineus asked.

"Romance at a time like *this*? If only love could conquer *Emperor Snake-breeder*." Caelifer thought.

The crowd, many members of which had been talking amongst themselves since the speech ended, now began to disperse. Arundineus, Caelifer and Pugna remained where they were.

"You want to visit my *house*? Are you sure we *know each other* well enough yet?" Pugna asked.

"The Emperor might be a tyrant, but courtship is not a crime. Hopefully, it never *will* be." Arundineus answered.

"What makes you think I gave you permission to start *courting* me?" Pugna asked.

"I am going to give myself permission to *stop listening*." Caelifer thought.

"I apologise for being so forward. I took a risk and it..." Arundineus answered.

"I do not love you, but I definitely do not *hate* you either. The gods have not forbidden us to speak to each other." Pugna said.

"If you were planning to visit her house, I suspect you were planning to do much more than *speak to each other*." Caelifer thought.

An amused expression appeared on Caelifer's face.

"What is with *him*?" Pugna asked.

"I could only *begin* to imagine." Arundineus answered.

"Is there something amusing about the idea of the gods forbidding us from speaking to each other?" Pugna asked.

"Something amusing? Maybe. I could only *begin* to

speculate." Caelifer answered.

"Shall we return to either our homes or places of work, then?" Arundineus asked.

Later that night, Arundineus was dreaming. In his dream, Emperor Colubrifer was standing near him holding a snake. The imaginary version of Emperor Colubrifer approached Arundineus's dream self and leaned over him, with his held snake close enough to bite Arundineus's neck.

"If traitors are snakes waiting to bite, then we shall bite *them* first." The imaginary version of the Emperor said.

"If we betray *tyranny*, we are not *truly* traitors." Arundineus's dream self said.

"If by tyranny I protect the Verian people from *greater* evils, then *obey* your tyrant protector." The imaginary version of the Emperor said.

"Tyranny does not make us better than the Cetin." Arundineus's dream self said.

"If tyranny protects us from the *Cetin*, what is the *difference*?" The imaginary version of the Emperor said.

Arundineus suddenly woke up, and was sweating profusely.

"His name may be *snake-haired*, but *literal* snakes? Are you not overplaying the drama, gods?" Arundineus said.

MISDIRECTION AND AGGRESSION

Several weeks later, Arundineus, Caelifer and Pugna were waiting at an imperial bakery.

"Have you heard the rumour the Emperor is planning something that requires the *highest degree of secrecy*?" Arundineus asked.

"Emperor Snake-skin is *always* planning something, *that* much is no secret." Caelifer answered.

"Is this a good bakery?" Arundineus asked.

"A *bad* bakery would go out of business, would it not?" Caelifer answered.

"How could any bakery be *bad*?" Pugna asked.

"A rat infestation, perhaps?" Caelifer answered.

"I assure you this bakery suffers no such affliction." A baker waiting to serve them said.

"Would not *every* bakery say that, though?" Caelifer said.

An imperial soldier a short distance away ran to approach Arundineus, Caelifer and Pugna.

"Are they *already* planning to imprison me for my jokes? Will they eventually make *smiling* illegal as well?" Caelifer asked.

"Maybe for people with *bad teeth*, at least." Pugna answered.

The imperial soldier became stationary about 5 metres from Arundineus, Caelifer and Pugna.

"Arundineus Vulgatus, Caelifer Credo, Pugna Prudentia, your presence is requested in the imperial palace." The imperial soldier said.

"Can you at least tell us *why*?" Arundineus asked.

"I was given strict instructions to relay the preceding message then return to duty. Good day to you all." The imperial soldier answered.

The imperial soldier nodded and partially bowed, then ran back in the direction he had arrived from.

"Living under tyranny yet an imperial soldier still manages to say 'good day' to us. Lucky *us*." Caelifer said.

Some indeterminate amount of time later, Arundineus, Caelifer and Pugna were standing in a room inside the imperial palace. A centurion stood in front of them.

"The three of you have been summoned as a group to maintain secrecy." The Centurion said.

"But if even *one* of us is a spy, how will anything you tell us remain *secret*?" Arundineus asked.

Caelifer pointed at the centurion.

"Perhaps *you* are a spy." Caelifer said.

"Perhaps *both* of us are spies. What *then*?" The Centurion said.

"Now you have me *stumped*." Caelifer said.

"If you *were* a spy, why would a spy *admit* to the possibility that they *are* a spy?" Arundineus asked.

"It is getting more and more difficult to figure out who

the spies are. *Precautions* are necessary, but they still might not be enough." The Centurion said.

"Spying is not a particularly loved profession…well, loved by the *enemy*, maybe." Caelifer said.

"The Cetin love their spies, and because a human stands out in Cetin territory, it is almost harder for *us* to spy on *them* than it is for *them* to spy on *us*." The Centurion said.

"How do they afford to buy off so many traitors to the Empire? They must avoid war because they cannot *afford* it." Pugna said.

"In any case, the three of you are to proceed to a place called Location Three and await further instructions." The Centurion said.

"Location Three? Where is *that*?" Arundineus asked.

"The whereabouts of Location Three are secret." The Centurion answered.

"If there are others being sent to *other* locations, can you at least tell us how many of those numbered locations there are?" Arundineus asked.

"That information is also secret. You may ask as many questions as you wish, but most I will not be allowed to answer truthfully." The Centurion answered.

"Has Emperor Hiss-face already made *telling the truth* a crime?" Caelifer thought.

"Location Three…perhaps the Emperor is planning an attack against the Cetin…*or* some rebel group." Arundineus said.

"You may speculate if you wish, but I am not allowed

to either confirm or deny any theories you might come up with." The Centurion said.

"This level of secrecy…maybe the Emperor is planning an invasion of Cetin territories. What does he hope to *gain*?" Arundineus thought.

"You will be escorted blindfolded to Location Three so as to minimise the chance of you revealing its where-abouts to the enemy, whether by intent or accidentally." The Centurion said.

"Would it be possible for us to speak with the Emperor shortly?" Arundineus asked.

"Non-essential communication with the Emperor has been restricted." The Centurion answered.

"Then take us to 'Location Three' and be done with it." Arundineus said.

"*That* request, at least, I am allowed to oblige." The Centurion said.

Two days later, Arundineus, Caelifer and Pugna, blind-folded, arrived by imperial escort in what looked to be a port city. A single imperial soldier removed Arundineus's blindfold, then Caelifer's blindfold, and lastly Pugna's blindfold.

"Do not wander too far, you will be receiving instruc-tions soon. Desertion will be considered a crime." The imperial soldier said.

"Why do you not simply tell what things will *not* be con-sidered a crime? Probably *much* easier." Caelifer thought.

"A port city? The Emperor *must* be planning an invasion.

I am not familiar with this city, though. Did they deliberately send us here knowing this city was unfamiliar to us?" Arundineus thought.

"Wait here. I must tend to my duties. If you are not here when I return, if you are captured, you will be promptly imprisoned. If you attempt to *evade* capture, you might be executed." The imperial soldier said.

"We understand. Duty does not wait." Arundineus said.

"*Sometimes* it does. *Time* is the thing that does not wait." The imperial soldier said.

The imperial soldier walked towards the nearby harbour and was quickly out of earshot of the group.

"Even if the Empire can afford war if the Cetin cannot, that does not mean the Empire should go ahead with it." Pugna said.

"We do not know for *certain* the Cetin cannot afford war." Arundineus said.

"The coins to pay all those spies have to come from *somewhere*." Pugna said.

"Who can say *if* or *when* the mystery of the Cetin economy will ever be solved?" Caelifer said.

"Let me guess – 'great thinkers have tried and failed'?" Arundineus asked.

"That *does* sound like something I would say, does it not?" Caelifer answered.

"'Wait here'. What if someone needs to relieve themselves?" Pugna said.

"Is Emperor Snake-venom in that much of a *hurry*? Is

his revenge *taking too long*?" Caelifer said.

"Even deciding his *invasion plans* probably took too long for him." Pugna said.

"How many other numbered locations do you think there are?" Arundineus asked.

"Too many for us to guess, probably too few to confuse the Cetin." Caelifer answered.

"Was that comment about someone relieving themselves general or were you suggesting a woman needs more privacy?" Arundineus asked.

Pugna blushed slightly.

"It was much more than a *suggestion*, Arundineus." Pugna answered.

"You must be starting to pick up humour from *Caelifer*." Arundineus said.

"How did she manage *that*? I did not *drop* my humour." Caelifer said.

"You never *do*, it seems." Arundineus said.

"Hopefully none of us will feel the need to *invade* a nearby building in search of a chamber pot before that guard returns." Caelifer said.

About three and a half hours later, the guard returned. Arundineus, Caelifer and Pugna were still in the general vicinity of where the guard had left them.

"New orders – you are to board the nearest ship and prepare to invade the Patrios continent. Your obedience is requested." The imperial soldier said.

"More like 'your obedience is *mandatory*'." Caelifer thought.

Later the following day, at night, Arundineus, Caelifer and Pugna were on board an imperial ship docked at the harbour. There was an entire fleet of imperial ships in the harbour, all loaded with soldiers.

"Patrios…straight into Cetin territory. The Cetin will not *forgive us* for this." Arundineus said.

"Now *you* are starting with the 'will not' statements?" Caelifer said.

"*Am* I? Let me know if I start talking like the Emperor." Arundineus said.

"I already *did*." Caelifer said.

"Even if, as Selene claimed, the Cetin do not *fear* violence, eventually they will *detest* it." Arundineus said.

"Some Cetin probably already *do* detest it." Pugna said.

"Anyone who told the Emperor his invasion plans are a bad idea is probably already dead. How *convenient*." Caelifer thought.

"When people are at sea on a ship, do they relieve themselves into the sea or are there multiple chamber pots on board?" Arundineus asked.

"Maybe a *man* might relieve himself into the sea, but a *woman* would expect a chamber pot." Pugna answered.

"What? How did that question manage to *not* gross her out?!" Caelifer thought.

"If only I could offer you a chamber pot…" Arundineus said, then whispered: "Instead of only offering my *heart*."

"If she is not moved by *that*, *nothing* you do will move her." Caelifer thought.

"Offer your heart? Is it not too early to be making romantic advances?" Pugna said.

"What would you suggest then, a romantic *retreat*?" Arundineus asked.

"If you failed to move her by offering your heart, you will definitely be *retreating* from this love battle. Love *war*? Or whatever what you two have is." Caelifer thought.

"Are you suggesting love is some kind of *battlefield*, Arundineus?" Pugna answered.

"It certainly *feels* like one." Arundineus said.

"Have you ever seen *Cupid* on a battlefield?" Pugna asked.

"If Cupid ever visits battlefields, it sounds like no one ever saw through his disguise. I mean, how many *archers* does the average army have?" Caelifer answered.

"I hope to never suffer the tragedy of falling in love on a battlefield." Arundineus said.

"Or falling in love *with* battle, or for *that* matter, falling *in* battle." Caelifer said.

"What *he* said." Arundineus said.

Pugna laughed.

"It must be getting late. I hear these kind of voyages are generally long and boring." Arundineus said.

"And you thought it was worth drawing attention to that fact *why*?" Caelifer said.

Pugna yawned.

"It is probably time to be thinking about getting to sleep. *We* will not be sleeping together, Arundineus…not until I know if we are a good match." Pugna said.

"How *will* you know?" Arundineus asked.

"What makes you so convinced we *are* a good match?" Pugna answered.

Pugna's expression changed to be a barely perceptible smile, then she walked in search of a cabin.

"Considering she used the phrase 'a good match' twice in less than as many minutes, I would wager you have a *good* chance." Caelifer said.

"How much would you *wager*?" Arundineus asked.

"Do people actually take the phrase 'I would wager' *literally*?" Caelifer answered.

"Some take too *many* things literally, including a certain *Legionaire*." Arundineus said.

Arundineus yawned.

"It will be weeks still before we make landfall on Patrios. Luckily there are *people to talk to*." Arundineus said.

Several weeks later, the ship, as well as the rest of the fleet that was in the harbour, was closing in on a landmass. There was no port in the vicinity, the fleet would need to anchor close to the beach.

"Patrios is just before us, men. Soon you will all fight for the glory of the Empire." The imperial soldier said.

"Are we at least going to be told what our target is?" Arundineus asked.

"Your target will be the inland city of Galinios. You are to capture rather than kill, as many enemies as possible." The imperial soldier said.

"Why would the Emperor want so many prisoners?" Arundineus asked.

"That is *his* business and not *yours*." The imperial soldier answered.

"Someone should close *Emperor Snake-slither's* business." Caelifer thought.

"You may be awarded a bonus for each enemy you successfully capture. Simply killing an enemy outright will *not* award any bonus." The imperial soldier said.

"I am not sure if I like where this is going." Arundineus thought.

"We will make landfall shortly, then march directly to Galinios. May the gods make you mighty!" The imperial soldier said.

Several days later, the army arrived outside the Cetin city of Galinios. It appeared lightly defended.

"Our forces will make short work of such pathetic defences. Conquer the city and capture as many enemies as possible! Do not disappoint the Emperor." The imperial soldier said.

"Too late to avoid the Emperor disappointing anyone *else*." Caelifer thought.

The imperial army marched towards Galinios and began their assault. The enemy appeared to be caught off-guard.

"Surrounding cities sent reinforcements to Megaleiodis because we were convinced the Verian Empire intended to attack the capital. Now some of those cities will almost certainly fall to the Empire." A Cetin male said in a language almost identical to Ancient Greek.

"Then I will make for the capital and warn them of our enemy's deception." Another Cetin male said in the same language.

The second of the two Cetin males to speak began running North. The imperial forces seemed too busy fighting to notice his escape. So far, the imperial forces were capturing a significant number of Cetin.

"Where are the Cetin's defenders? Anyone would think the Cetin were strangers to violence." An imperial soldier said.

"Sanctus does not forbid killing demons. Kill as many of the demons as you can!" A second imperial soldier said.

"If you fail to capture any enemies, you forfeit the bonus they mentioned." The first imperial soldier said.

"And miss out on the opportunity to *kill demons*? Never!" The second imperial soldier said.

The second imperial soldier rushed towards a slightly muscular Cetin male and attacked. The Cetin male was armed with a short sword and parried his opponent's attacks.

"Hurry up and *die*, demon!" The second imperial soldier said.

"Watch out for the renowned *killer* of demons…no, wait, watch out for the renowned killer *demon*." The Slightly Muscular Cetin said.

The slightly muscular Cetin male parried an attack from his opponent, then kicked his opponent in his left leg, which knocked his opponent off-balance. He then unleashed a flurry of sword attacks. The bloodthirsty soldier fell to the ground and began bleeding out.

"I hope *I* never become that eager to kill." Arundineus said.

"Unless it is *Emperor Snake-stealer*. Hopefully someone is *that* eager to kill *him*, at least." Caelifer thought.

The imperial forces were sweeping through the town with almost no serious resistance.

"To think some of us in the Empire are *afraid* of Cetin. How can you be afraid of an enemy that fights so poorly?" An imperial archer said.

"Either this is a trap or we caught them off-guard. They must have thought we would attack their capital directly. It seems *they* were the ones who were afraid." A second imperial archer said.

Several imperial soldiers who carried lit torches approached nearby Cetin houses and performed arson. Some frightened female Cetin as well as some Cetin children fled their burning residences.

"Burn, demons! The only fate good enough for you." One of the torch-carrying soldiers said.

"When was *arson* part of our invasion strategy?" Pugna asked.

"You realise we have all but declared war on the Cetin, do you not? Have you never *heard* of 'the fires of war'?" Caelifer answered.

"I thought it was only a figure of speech." Pugna said.

"I wonder if *any* expression related to war is *ever* only a figure of speech." Arundineus said.

The imperial forces advanced further into the town.

"Watch those wretched demons burn!" An imperial soldier said.

"You could hardly accuse him of not taking this war *seriously enough*." Caelifer said.

"How much more seriously *can* he take it?" Arundineus asked.

Three imperial soldiers advanced on the slightly muscular male Cetin who killed the bloodthirsty soldier and attacked, but were soundly defeated.

"You fought not a man; you fought a killer demon." The Slightly Muscular Cetin said.

Arundineus approached the Cetin male.

"Do you mind if *I* fight this supposed 'killer demon'?" Arundineus asked.

"I will not fight like a man; I will fight like a demon." The Slightly Muscular Cetin said.

"*I* might fight like a demon as well. You *might* defeat me, but if you fight me, you risk rousing a mysterious power I have and *you* might be defeated instead." Arundineus said.

"I will take my chances if it is all the same to *you*." The Slightly Muscular Cetin said.

Arundineus and the Slightly Muscular Cetin engaged each other in combat. There was no sign of Arundineus's mysterious power having activated.

"Tell me about this *mysterious power* I risked rousing." The Slightly Muscular Cetin said.

"If it awakens, there will be no mistaking it – awakening it *would* be the mistake." Arundineus said.

"We shall see." The Slightly Muscular Cetin said.

Arundineus attacked his opponent, who easily parried the blow then slashed his left arm.

"Will your hidden talent awaken in time to prevent you dying?" The Slightly Muscular Cetin said.

"Do you *want* it to?" Arundineus asked.

Arundineus attacked again, but his opponent parried yet again, then slashed the right side of Arundineus's torso. Arundineus was beginning to tire.

"Do we *need* to do this?" Arundineus asked.

"Did your people *need* to invade?" The Slightly Muscular Cetin answered.

"Did that rhetorical question *need* to be asked?" Arundineus asked.

Suddenly, Arundineus's familiar mysterious power activated. His eyes turned scarlet again and his red aura returned.

"I would not be mistaken to think *this* is the power you mentioned, would I?" The Slightly Muscular Cetin asked.

"If you value your life, you will flee." Arundineus answered.

Arundineus launched into a flurry of sword strikes. The Slightly Muscular Cetin blocked, parried, or dodged most of them, but a final sword strike hit him across the stomach.

"Are you sure you want to risk your life for a slim chance to defeat me?" Arundineus asked.

"What is that power? *I* was not the killer demon; it was *you* all along." The Slightly Muscular Cetin answered.

"*I* can keep fighting if *you* can." Arundineus said.

"Perhaps I *do* value my life, *after all*." The Slightly Muscular Cetin said.

The Slightly Muscular Cetin bowed, then fled.

"Was that a battle between two men, or two *demons*?" Caelifer asked.

"How do you want me to *answer* that question?" Arundineus asked.

That night, the imperial forces had successfully captured the town with minimal losses. A large group of prisoners were tied up in the middle of a wide street.

"*Some* lucky soldiers might be making *a good income* from Cetin-hunting. *I* say, 'if you want to profit off creating misfortune, go ahead'." Caelifer said.

"I hope that was sarcasm." Arundineus said.

"Of course. Profiting from misfortune is unfortunate." Caelifer said.

"Unfortunate for the *Cetin*, at least." Pugna said.

A commander approached the group of prisoners.

"We have done *well*, very well indeed. Long live the Emperor!" The commander said.

"*I* prefer 'soon die the tyrant'." Caelifer thought.

"Today, *one* Cetin town fell, eventually even the Cetin capital will fall." The commander said.

"You sound very certain - are you the proud owner of a *crystal ball*, perhaps? Perhaps you should have instead said 'eventually the Cetin capital *might* fall. Who cares if you said a particular thing *might* happen but did not?" Caelifer thought.

"Demons deserve *pain*. We shall make sure they receive *more* than they can handle." An imperial soldier said.

"Today, the Verian Empire fell into a moral abyss, and we do not even know where the bottom of it is yet." Arundineus thought.

The Verian Empire launched a full-scale invasion shortly after capturing Galinios. The Cetin informant arrived safely in Megaleiodis, but a considerable number more Cetin towns were captured, and *many* more Cetin taken prisoner by the time the Cetin were able to mobilise sufficient reinforcements. The Verian Empire was truly in the throes of a rapid downward spiral, but the moral abyss would prove to be far deeper than even Arundineus had imagined.

The Emperor's advisors had devised a clever deception that caught the Cetin off-guard, but mutual mistrust would give way to deep loathing. Persecution is not a solid foundation to build deep friendships or alliances upon. The roots of the Cetin's persecution were deep and complex. Terrible though Emperor Colubrifer may have been in his own right, many shared more than a few of his views about the Cetin, perhaps a truth even *more* terrible.

But it was perhaps still only the *beginning* of the downward spiral...

THE FRUITS OF TYRANNY

45 years passed. Most of the Cetin taken prisoner during the Empire's invasion were sent to internment camps with appalling conditions, and a small number were killed outright. Arundineus and Caelifer, who had both almost fully greyed, stood in a large internment camp. About one third of the Cetin prisoners were emaciated.

"Are prisoners supposed to look so thin?" Arundineus asked.

"Troublemakers forfeit food until they stop causing trouble." An Imperial Soldier said.

"Assuming they do not *die* first. Of course, if *anyone* deserves to starve, it would be Emperor Snake-fang." Caelifer thought.

"Cetin may be capable of starvation, but true demons are not." Arundineus said.

"That does not prove Cetin are *not* demons, though." The Imperial Soldier said.

"Is it like this in the *other* internment camps?" Arundineus asked.

"Some might be worse; some might be better." The Imperial Soldier answered.

"Somebody hurry up and send Emperor Snake-fang to an internment camp *worse* than this one and put him on barely survivable rations *immediately*!" Caelifer thought.

"Surely the ones who are starving complain of hunger?" Arundineus asked.

"If they *do*, we can barely understand whatever language it is they speak. It certainly does not sound like the Cetin language we *know*." The Imperial Soldier answered.

"You sound like you barely understand *anything* about the Cetin. Why should being barely able to understand their *language* be any kind of surprise?" Caelifer thought.

"How many internment camps have the Cetin built on Patrios? Are *they* treating us the same way we are treating these *prisoners*?" Arundineus asked.

"Patrios is no longer a threat. If you want to *help* these prisoners, only orders directly from the Emperor will change anything. You would have to convince him to *change his mind* first, of course." The Imperial Soldier answered.

"First I would have to convince myself trying to convince him was a *good idea*." Arundineus said.

An imperial messenger arrived and approached Arundineus and Caelifer.

"Arundineus Vulgatus and Caelifer Credo, Emperor Colubrifer requests your presence." The Imperial Messenger said.

"You might have a chance to change his mind *after all*." The Imperial Soldier said.

"We could get him to *change his mind* about *tyranny*,

or he could change his mind about *letting us live*." Caelifer thought.

"Do you require an escort to the imperial palace?" The Imperial Messenger asked.

"Is it a *choice* or was an escort *requested*?" Arundineus answered.

"The Emperor is not one to abide refusal." The Imperial Messenger said.

"He is also not one to abide *moral decency*, yet we treat it like a badly-kept secret." Caelifer thought.

Several days later, Arundineus and Caelifer were again in the same room of the imperial palace where they and Pugna had received instructions from a centurion. Emperor Colubrifer slowly entered the room. He was fully greyed and badly wrinkled, and appeared hideous compared to in his youth. He clutched a walking stick.

"*That* is the terrible tyrant people are so afraid to disobey? The Emperor is practically a *prune* now. Oh, the jokes I could tell looking at him *now*!" Caelifer thought.

"Arundineus, Caelifer, you have been…" Emperor Colubrifer said.

"What? Caught having a sense of humour?" Caelifer thought.

"Sorry, my mind is not as sharp as it used to be." Emperor Colubrifer said.

"*Sharp*?! Is *that* what you thought your mind was?" Caelifer thought.

"Please, Emperor, continue." Arundineus said.

"Your loyalty to the Empire has been considerable. I hear there is a lack of compliance in the internment camps." Emperor Colubrifer said.

"Cetin *breathing without your permission* would count as a 'lack of compliance' in *your* estimation." Caelifer thought.

"Do you have orders, Emperor?" Arundineus asked.

"None worth *following*, if I had to guess." Caelifer thought.

The Emperor pondered.

"Whichever internment camp has the least amount of compliance...make an example of any Cetin prisoners who *defy* us." Emperor Colubrifer said.

"Whoever defies *you* I would consider heroic." Caelifer thought.

"What exactly do you mean by 'make an example'?" Arundineus asked.

"Do you want him to give you examples of *how* to make an example of someone? You *do* realise he is a *tyrant*, do you not, or do you need *examples* of tyrants?" Caelifer thought.

"Use your imagination. Apparently *forfeiting food* is not enough to make the more defiant prisoners fall in line. More *creative* punishment is required." Emperor Colubrifer said.

"Apparently, *imagination* is something you sorely lack. Sorry, I meant a *conscience* is something you sorely lack." Caelifer thought.

"What would be a more creative punishment than withholding food?" Arundineus asked.

"Forget a more creative punishment, make it more

brutal instead." Emperor Colubrifer answered.

"More brutal…I think I understand." Arundineus said.

"And *I* think I understand that just when we think we have seen the full extent of your tyranny, your tyranny reveals itself to have more layers than an onion." Caelifer thought.

"You have been rather quiet, Caelifer. Have you anything to add?" Emperor Colubrifer asked.

"Nothing comes immediately to mind." Caelifer answered.

"Very well, you have received your orders. I trust neither of you object?" Emperor Colubrifer said.

"What would *you* know about trust, except maybe how to *abuse* it?" Caelifer thought.

Emperor Colubrifer began breathing heavily.

"My body betrays me. Leave me." Emperor Colubrifer said.

"Your conscience betrayed you *long* ago, your body is simply catching up." Caelifer thought.

Arundineus and Caelifer were on horseback, led by a single legionnaire on horseback.

"What do you think the gods think about tyranny?" Arundineus asked.

"Are you kidding? Some people think the gods themselves *are* tyrants. *I* disagree – why would you worship tyrants? What about our good Emperor? If he worships gods, it would be a case of a tyrant worshipping tyrants. A rather *comforting* thought, would you not agree?" Caelifer answered.

"Is it safe to be talking about these kinds of things so *openly*?" Arundineus asked.

"If you *shouted*, our guide *might* hear you, but you were not *planning* on doing that, were you?" Caelifer answered.

"*Good* Emperor? It is getting more and more difficult to see how there is even a *shred* of goodness in that man." Arundineus said.

"Even just hearing that phrase 'good Emperor' is enough to make me shudder – he is not even so much as a *decent* Emperor. Emperor Colubrifer is certainly a *bad apple*, and I want to hope there are still some *good* apples on the Verian tree." Caelifer said.

"There must be a *worm* in that particular apple." Arundineus said.

"I certainly *respect* him about as much as a worm." Caelifer thought.

"Worms at least are mostly harmless." Arundineus said.

"Harmless is what a certain Emperor would like his *enemies* to be." Caelifer said.

Later, inside one of the internment camps, Arundineus and Caelifer were being led by an imperial soldier. About three-fifths of the prisoners were emaciated.

"Even withholding food did not prevent prisoners rebelling. Some have already *died* for their insolence." The imperial soldier said.

"Did you not have the courage to say they were murdered? Please forgive prisoners for not being more *embracing* of Emperor Bad Apple's glorious tyranny." Caelifer thought.

"Hopefully those who died were mostly from starvation." Arundineus said.

"You want to be *hopeful* about prisoners dying from starvation instead of murder? Is anyone aware how *crazy* this situation is?" Caelifer thought.

"I do not care *how* many we have to kill. To be honest, withholding food *costs* us less." The imperial soldier said.

"I have new orders from the Emperor. He wants you to use more *brutal* methods of controlling the prisoners." Arundineus said.

"I would be pleased to oblige. The prisoners cannot be allowed to consider us *merciful*." The imperial soldier said.

"What makes you think there is any risk of prisoners considering you *merciful*? Any belief in Deus Benevolus would be snuffed out quickly if your roles were reversed." Caelifer thought.

"Are there any...what is the correct word...*influential* prisoners?" Arundineus asked.

"One's sphere of influence must be wide indeed to reach outside a prison." Caelifer thought.

"I can *show* you one, if you will show me some of the *brutal methods* that you had in mind." The imperial soldier answered.

"I hope this is not something I will regret later." Arundineus thought.

The imperial soldier led Arundineus and Caelifer to a Cetin man, who was definitely not emaciated, with larger than average horns. The Cetin man's hands were tied by rope.

"We should have withheld food from you when we had the chance." The imperial soldier said.

"My people will not forget your recent injustices." The Cetin man said.

"Your people are no longer a threat to the Empire." The imperial soldier said.

"Or so your tyrant Emperor would have you believe." The Cetin man said.

Arundineus inhaled then exhaled.

"I cannot believe it has come to this." Arundineus said.

"That it has come to *what*? Our *own* people conveniently forgetting *our* recent injustices?" Caelifer thought.

Arundineus grabbed the Cetin man's horns.

"These horns are precious to you, I take it?" Arundineus asked.

"Am I supposed to deny feeling an *attachment* to my horns? Would *you* deny an attachment to your fingernails?" The Cetin man said.

"A horned Cetin values their horns as much as fingernails?" Arundineus thought.

"Soldier, do any of our soldiers here have an axe or know where they can get one?" Arundineus asked.

"Ah! You mean to *behead* the prisoner. That is cruelty I can *support*!" The imperial soldier answered.

"The one who has lost their head around here is *you*." Caelifer thought.

"That was not quite an actual *answer* to my question." Arundineus said.

"I had better fetch an axe before the Emperor decides *I* should be the one to be beheaded." The imperial soldier said.

"A pity there is no way of arranging for the *Emperor* to be beheaded instead." Caelifer thought.

An unknown amount of time later, the imperial soldier returned holding an axe. He approached Arundineus.

"Axes are less common than I thought. I want to see his head roll!" The imperial soldier said.

"No, I want to see *your* head roll, or better yet, *the Emperor's!*" Caelifer thought.

"Did you think axes were *common*?" Arundineus asked.

"The Empire needs a tax to fund more axes." The imperial soldier answered.

"More like the Empire needs to take an axe to taxes." Caelifer said.

"Instead of a tax *for* axes, you would prefer we attack taxes *with* an axe?" The imperial soldier asked.

"Yes, I do. One way you *pay* more money, the other you *keep* more money." Caelifer answered.

"Take the axe. Peptonax has kept his head too long as it is." The imperial soldier said.

"Peptonax…the unfamiliar language must be some kind of combination of the Cetin language and Verian. How then does he speak Verian *fluently*?" Arundineus thought.

The imperial soldier passed the axe to Arundineus.

"Deus Benevolus, have mercy on this ruffian." Arundineus said.

Arundineus swung the axe, chopping off significant parts of Peptonax's horns. He then shifted the axe to his left hand, and with his right hand, Arundineus picked up the fragments of Peptonax's horns and handed them to him.

"Consider it a reminder of the consequences of resisting the Empire." Arundineus said.

"Thank you for your...*generosity*. The only gift I can give you at such short notice is my contempt." Peptonax said.

"Otherwise known as 'the only gift worth giving' to his oppressors." Caelifer thought.

"Soldier, how does Peptonax speak Verian so fluently? I was told some new language had developed among the prisoners." Arundineus said.

"He used to be a *translator* before he developed a rebellious streak." The imperial soldier said.

"A translator? Well done, Peptonax, you have earned my respect." Arundineus said.

"For all the good it will do me in *these* circumstances." Peptonax said.

"Peptonax should not give you any more trouble. Are there problems in any of the *other* internment camps?" Arundineus asked.

"Rampant starvation, for *one* thing." Caelifer thought.

"You will be informed of any pressing developments." The imperial soldier said.

"Which will not include news of *starvation* being abolished." Caelifer thought.

The imperial soldier bowed then walked away.

"What has been going on in your mind lately, Caelifer?" Arundineus asked.

"Things too dangerous to discuss openly." Caelifer answered.

"In your case, *jokes* too dangerous to speak openly." Arundineus said.

"Careful, my humour is supposed to be a secret." Caelifer said.

"Is it, though?" Arundineus asked.

"The Emperor either does not know or does not care." Caelifer answered.

"He might simply be turning a blind eye." Arundineus said.

"If only he had a literal blind eye. His *leadership* lacks a certain vision, at least." Caelifer said.

"That it does. Should we ask if any of the other camps need our help?" Arundineus asked.

"I am tempted to say we should *not*." Caelifer answered.

Some unknown length of time later, Arundineus and Caelifer were in a different internment camp. In this particular camp, the starvation problem seemed especially dire.

"Four-fifths of the prisoners are so starved they are barely clinging to life, yet they *still* will not yield to us." An imperial soldier said.

"If you let four-fifths of this camp's prisoners die of starvation, you are at least *partially* responsible." Arundineus said.

"The prisoners have discovered that if they go without

food, they have no reason to obey us." The imperial soldier said.

"If only the Verian Empire had 'no reason' to obey a certain nameless Emperor." Caelifer thought.

"Do all of them only speak that new language, or are there any translators among them?" Arundineus asked.

"There is one we specifically make sure is well-fed for that very reason." The imperial soldier answered.

"Will you please *introduce* me to said translator?" Arundineus asked.

"I do not see any way you could make the situation any *worse*." The imperial soldier answered.

"Not much of a vote of confidence, but I will take it." Arundineus said.

"Follow me." The imperial soldier said.

The imperial soldier led Arundineus and Caelifer to a restrained yellow-eyed Cetin man with horns curved like scimitars.

"To what do I owe this…what is the opposite of pleasure? Agony, perhaps?" The Cetin man said.

"Soldier, what is the translator's name?" Arundineus asked.

"Topomere." The imperial soldier said.

"Topomere, I beg you, stop this madness!" Arundineus said.

"Your Empire is led by an insane tyrant, yet you accuse *me* of madness?" Topomere said.

"Our Empire is led by an insane tyrant…clearly *you* understand. When can we get together and *share* what we have discovered?" Caelifer thought.

"How does allowing some of your people to die unnecessarily help further the Cetin cause?" Arundineus asked.

"If we lose our will to oppose your corrupt Empire, what good does the prisoners living do us?" Topomere answered.

"Could you not have at least uttered something memorable like, 'Let us die free that we shall not live as slaves'?" Arundineus said.

"Better not let the *Emperor* hear about that." Caelifer thought.

Topomere appeared to ponder.

"My people will rejoice when news of the Emperor's death comes to pass. If our gods are vengeful, I hope his decline is excruciating." Topomere said.

"You might be waiting longer than you think for *that* news. His decline has *already* been excruciating – his *moral* decline, that is." Caelifer thought.

"I do not know what I can offer you. Even freeing those of your people in the internment camps would have to be approved by the Emperor himself." Arundineus said.

"If you do not know what you can offer me, then *I* do not know why I am talking to you." Topomere said.

"If the Emperor dies…" Arundineus said.

"That is not an 'if', but a 'when'." Topomere said.

"When the Emperor dies, it might be possible to arrange for prisoners to be released from the internment camps." Arundineus said.

"Perhaps you can explain so I do not misunderstand – I take it you are not yourself offering to *kill* the Emperor?" Topomere said.

"What do you think they would do to me if I *did*?" Arundineus asked.

"You have not given me a compelling reason to talk to you." Topomere answered.

"You might have given yourself a compelling reason to kill the *Emperor*, though." Caelifer thought.

"You might not have to wait as long as you think for the Emperor to die – his age is *advanced*." Arundineus said.

"It might also please you to know at his age how hideous he is." Caelifer said.

"Old and hideous…now, if he could just be *dead* and *harmless*, my people could celebrate." Topomere said.

"*Your* people can celebrate after ours have become tired of even the *idea* of celebrating, or until anyone's *employment* is threatened." Caelifer thought.

Suddenly, Arundineus's mysterious power awakened. In his strengthened state, his left hand grabbed Topomere's right shoulder, seemingly of its own accord.

"Was the 'harmless' part too much?" Topomere said.

"Why did I grab you?" Arundineus asked.

"Do you mean that was *not* deliberate? Having red eyes is normal for *my* people, not so much for *yours*." Topomere said.

"It is not like *me* to suddenly lose self-control." Arundineus said.

"He still has better self-control than the *Emperor*. Losing self-control is practically one of the Emperor's *character traits*." Caelifer thought.

"Should I be starting to be worried at this point?" Topomere asked.

"Only if you anger me – in this state, even I would not like *myself* if I was angry." Arundineus answered.

"Show me a *likeable* angry person. No, really." Caelifer said.

"No offense intended, but how am I supposed to if you are angry? Seeing red may be associated with anger, but in *this* situation, that might not be so useful." Topomere said.

Arundineus's left hand squeezed Topomere's right shoulder. Arundineus struggled against himself to release his grip.

"I have heard of wrestling against oneself, I did not expect to see it happen to someone *literally*." Topomere said.

"Where is that man learning all his *jokes*?" Caelifer thought.

Arundineus struggled against himself again, this time with greater determination. He managed to force himself to release his grip on Topomere, but the strengthened state remained.

"You have made your point. I will convince the other prisoners to obey the guards." Topomere said.

"This…*outburst* was not intentional." Arundineus said.

"Regardless of that, your point has been made." Topomere said.

"I know so little about this mysterious power." Arundineus said.

"Perhaps giving it a name would help. 'Outburst' would not quite be such a terrible name." Topomere said.

"Are you trying to suggest I should ask you to *forgive* an outburst?" Arundineus asked.

"Forgive an outburst – for the Emperor, that notion is practically *unthinkable*." Caelifer thought.

"I think our business is concluded. I should not have been so foolish as to get my hopes up." Topomere answered.

"What were you expecting me to *do*?" Arundineus asked.

"It does not matter, dying for one's freedom sounds poetic, but I was never much *good* at poetry." Topomere answered.

"I apologise, Topomere, someone who is no lover of tyranny should have had something valuable to offer you." Arundineus said.

"'Lover of Tyranny' is probably one of the titles history will give old Colubrifer." Caelifer thought.

"Why do I get the impression you have been secretly making jokes, Caelifer?" Arundineus asked.

"Experience, perhaps?" Caelifer answered.

"If only I could *hear* what goes on in that mind of yours." Arundineus said.

"A phrase I hope is never uttered by the Emperor." Caelifer said.

Some unknown amount of time later, Caelifer was

dreaming. In his dream, Emperor Colubrifer was standing in front of a large chest full of snakes.

"Is *that* where you have been hiding your snakes?" Caelifer said.

"I should perhaps thank you, Caelifer, you have demonstrated why I should never have made the mistake of forgetting to make humour illegal." The dream version of Emperor Colubrifer said.

"You should never have made the mistake of forgetting to have a conscience, *either*, but what can you do?" Caelifer said.

"What can I do? Perhaps live up to the name 'Emperor Snake-fang'? Guards, bring him to me!" Emperor Colubrifer said.

In the dream, two nearby imperial guards each grabbed Caelifer by one of his shoulders and dragged him over to the Emperor. The Emperor reached into the chest of snakes and pulled out a snake.

"I truly should have been more *embracing* of that whole snake theme, should not have I?" The dream version of Emperor Colubrifer said.

Caelifer suddenly woke up. He looked tired.

"Just once could the gods at least be generous enough to give me a dream where the Emperor *dies*?" Caelifer said.

FREEDOM'S LABOURS

At the entrance to one of the Verian Empire's internment camps, a man dressed in drab clothes was approaching a military checkpoint. An imperial soldier gestured for the man to stop.

"Identify yourself and state your purpose." The imperial soldier said.

"In short order, but I fear you will not *approve* of my purpose." The drably-dressed man said.

"Are you intending to cause trouble?" The imperial soldier asked.

"I am intending to cause *rebellion*. I am intending to cause the *freedom* of many." The drably-dressed man answered.

"Then the Empire should *in short order* see fit to cause your *death*." The imperial soldier said.

"Or I could see fit to cause death to anyone who stands in my way." The drably-dressed man said.

"Kill the intruder!" The imperial soldier said.

The imperial soldier brandished his sword and attempted to attack the drably-dressed man. As soon as his sword got anywhere close to landing a blow, the imperial soldier was knocked back a considerable distance.

"But you were undefended!" The imperial soldier said.

"If you take defending so seriously, I must take *attacking* even more seriously." The drably-dressed man said.

"Guards, kill the intruder no matter what it takes!" The imperial soldier said.

"Do you intend to offer me a challenge?" The drably-dressed man said.

Archers took position in a nearby watchtower and prepared to shoot.

"Die, intruder!" One of the archers in the watchtower said.

The archers began shooting the drably-dressed man. Their arrows came close to him, but disintegrated before reaching his skin.

"Be careful, he is some kind of magician." Another of the archers in the watchtower said.

"Indeed, but have you any magicians nearby? If not, simply realising I have magic is of little consequence to you." The drably-dressed man said.

"Keep shooting! Eventually his magic will fail." The first of the archers who spoke said.

The archers in the watchtower prepared another volley of arrows.

"I suppose I should leave an *impression* of some kind. How *else* will I be remembered?" The drably-dressed man said.

The drably-dressed man appeared to concentrate, then summoned an ornately dressed ethereal archer who wielded a golden bow, who hovered in mid-air between him and the watchtower.

"This is not possible!" The second of the archers in the watchtower to speak said.

"The 'not' part of that sentence is not correct." The drably-dressed man said.

"First he has some kind of magical shield, now he has some kind of spirit archer? How do we not know who he *is*?" The second archer asked.

"Sagittarius, kill any archers you find in this camp." The drably-dressed man said.

The ethereal archer obeyed, and shot an exploding arrow that killed the archers in the watchtower with a single shot. Sagittarius then flew above the internment camp, scanning to see if he could locate more archers. He then noticed multiple archers spread throughout the internment camp.

"There are a considerable number of remaining archers, Heros. They will require more than a single arrow." Sagittarius said.

"Let none of them escape, but avoid damaging the internment camp - there should be green-skinned prisoners I should like to free." Heros said.

"Yes, of *those*, there are many." Sagittarius said.

"Kill all the men in Verian uniforms, kill *none* of the green men." Heros said.

"Even the men armed with only swords? What have I to fear from swords?" Sagittarius asked.

"Have you forgotten about the green men already?"

Heros answered.

"It would seem I *had*." Sagittarius said.

Verian archers took aim at Sagittarius.

"Unleash your full fury on the enemy!" A commander said.

"I was not aware our arrows were capable of harming ghosts." An Imperial Archer said.

"What about the men with swords?" A soldier armed with a sword asked.

"Throw them at the enemy." The commander answered.

"Throw a sword at a flying ghost? Are you *hearing* yourself?" The soldier armed a sword said.

"We will not be reporting to the Emperor that an entire internment camp full of soldiers abandoned their posts on account of a *ghost*." The commander said.

"But…" The soldier armed with a sword said.

"But *nothing*, or I will make sure that is all that remains of your *reputation*." The commander said.

The soldier armed with a sword gulped.

"Orders are orders, I suppose." The soldier said.

The Imperial archers fired a volley of arrows. Sagittarius dodged almost all of them, but one arrow passed through his left foot.

"See? If weapons pass through, the enemy *must* be a ghost." The Imperial Archer said.

"Does being proven true grant you any specific advantage in this battle?" The commander asked.

"It grants me *satisfaction*, at least." The Imperial Archer said.

The commander grumbled.

"If my foes have multiplied, then so shall my arrows." Sagittarius said.

Sagittarius waved his left hand over his bow, and his arrow multiplied into a horizontal row of arrows from left to right in front of him, numbering nine. He shot the single arrow that was actually in his bow, and the newly created arrows also shot off, homing in on nearby Imperial archers. Each targeted archer was hit – most somewhere not in any way life-threatening, such as a foot or hand, but two archers were each hit in different parts of the torso. One of the two archers had attempted to run and was hit in the back.

"Who is that demon and why is he helping the enemy?" The commander asked.

"Your definition of 'demon' is rather *broad*, is it not?" Sagittarius answered.

"Fire at will. If there is even a ghost of a chance of wounding that enemy, I want him at *our* mercy." The commander said.

"Your *words* do not wound me *enough*?" Sagittarius said.

The Imperial archers took aim and each prepared another arrow. The archers' accuracy seemed to have improved, as this time about half of the arrows fired by the archers reached and passed through Sagittarius.

"How long can your men *survive* this back-and-forth game?" Sagittarius asked.

"Is there a hell for traitors to the Empire?" The commander answered.

"I should hope not even your *reigning tyrant* is sent to such a place. Though 'hell' might be something he has been *creating*." Sagittarius said.

"Fire until either your arrows run out or you die." The commander said.

The commander laughed.

"Maybe those of you who *do* die can give him a proper fight as ghosts." The commander said.

Sagittarius created another horizontal row of arrows.

"You could have at least provided a challenge." Sagittarius said.

"*You* are the challenge, and you presume to *complain*?" The commander said.

Sagittarius shot his arrows, which again homed in on Imperial archers. Each archer was hit in their bow-pulling hand and were no longer able to use a bow. Some of the Imperial archers even dropped their bows.

"So you will kill all of my men just to save a small number of worthless Cetin?" The commander asked.

"Preferably, I would take away their ability to fight rather than take their lives. As for a phrase such as 'worthless Cetin' – are you truly so sure of your *own* worth?" Sagittarius answered.

"If I cannot hurt *you*, then I will simply kill the prisoners instead. Men, whoever is able, set fire to this internment camp then flee. Kill any prisoners who escape the camp. If someone *summoned* that ghost, find them and *kill* them." The commander said.

"How have I resisted the urge to kill *you*?" Sagittarius said.

Most of the archers begin to flee despite their injuries. The commander laughed in a maniacal manner.

"Those prisoners will not survive the night. They shall have no salvation from any of *your* efforts." The commander said.

"*You* are probably more afraid of death than the prisoners are. What will be *your* salvation?" Sagittarius said.

"If you were summoned here, your master will die before nightfall." The commander said.

"Why has no one looked for whoever summoned the ghost? If there is a magician nearby controlling the ghost, I want the magician dismembered." The commander said.

"Heros, the guards might come searching for you soon. You had best have a plan to defend yourself, it is too late to outrun them." Sagittarius said telepathically (without moving his mouth).

"Wait, could the magician be in *that* direction? Remember, the magician is to be dismembered. Do not return without a piece of his body. Whoever brings me the magician's manhood will receive a promotion." The commander said.

The remaining able-bodied archers and swordsmen began running in the direction of the camp's entrance.

"Heros, either you have an Animus to summon capable of handling these guards, or this rescue mission has now become a suicide mission." Sagittarius said.

Near the entrance to the camp, Heros stretched. The

guards were almost in view of him.

"I will need to summon another Animus in order to attack, but I will not be able to sustain my magical barrier and summon an Animus at the same time. The guards are not yet in position…I act *now* or not at all. Strong defence… Scorpio." Heros thought.

Heros concentrated, and a creature that was a hybrid of a man and a scorpion was summoned.

"Heros…to what do I owe this pleasure?" Scorpio asked.

"See those guards running towards us? I need sturdy defence." Heros answered.

"Hard Carapace!" Scorpio said.

A black armour covered Heros's clothes.

Of the guards, the archers among them were finally in firing range of Heros. The archers took aim.

"Is this all tyranny could muster to oppose us?" Scorpio asked.

"Eliminate the magician at all costs – without *him*, his summons have no master." The commander said.

The Imperial archers let loose a volley of arrows. Some hit Scorpio and bounced off his carapace, while most hit Heros but were repelled.

"What vile magic have you consorted with?" The commander asked.

"What vile tyrant have *you* consorted with?" Heros answered.

Scorpio lunged at the archers and thrusted his tail. An unfortunate archer was eliminated almost immediately.

"Have you no method of attack without your summons?" The commander asked.

"I do not believe *in* wasteful use of magic." Heros answered.

"I do not believe in the use of magic." The commander said.

"I have been well-acquainted with *your* particular prejudices." Heros said.

Scorpio attacked the archers wildly, rapidly thinning their numbers. A few sword-wielding guards took turns in attacking Scorpio, to no avail.

"Have you forgotten I need only call and Sagittarius can assist Scorpio in defeating your men?" Heros asked.

"You have forgotten perhaps the most *important* thing: loyalty to the Empire." The commander answered.

"If anything, Sagittarius was probably holding back when he fought your men. If I were you, I would hate to see how he fights when he is *determined*." Heros said.

"You will see how *I* fight when *I* am determined." The commander said.

"I have seen *you* fight. Unless you call your efforts so far 'holding back'?" Heros said.

Scorpio fought several Imperial swordsmen simultaneously and was not at all at a disadvantage. By now, Scorpio was beginning to close in on the commander.

"Have you forgotten the taste of freedom?" Heros asked.

"I was not aware freedom had a flavour." The commander answered.

"If *tyranny* has a flavour, it must be some kind of slow-acting poison. Disguise the taste of poison all you want; it is still just as deadly." Heros said.

"Tyranny is worse than any poison *I* secrete." Scorpio said.

"Scorpio, Sagittarius…why not simply summon the *entire* zodiac to defeat me?" The commander said.

"I doubt any magician alive could summon the entire zodiac at the same time." Heros said.

"That bodes well for the Empire." The commander said.

"Do you know how hard it would have been for me to arrange for eleven other magicians to meet me here and each summon one of the signs of the zodiac? If you hate me so much, you would have *detested* an entire group of zodiac magicians." Heros said.

"Then there *are* zodiac magicians!" The commander said.

"Is that the *point* you think I was trying to make?" Heros said.

The remaining Imperial swordsman huddled around the commander, and formed a physical barrier. There were very few Imperial archers present who were still capable of fighting.

"I give you one final chance to surrender and willingly free your prisoners." Heros said.

"I will not surrender to someone who summons *ghosts* to fight for him." The commander said.

"Then you are complicit with Colubrifer's tyranny. I believe in what *I* fight for." Heros said.

"Heros, why have you not called Sagittarius here?" Scorpio asked.

"Do we even *need* his help at this point? There is not a single enemy magician in the entire camp. Twelve zodiac magicians would have easily captured the camp in mere minutes." Heros answered.

"The enemy commander's distrust of magic seems to have worked to our advantage." Scorpio said.

"Is *that* all I needed? More magic?" The commander said.

"A little too late to be getting ideas, would you not agree?" Heros said.

Scorpio finished off the remaining archers, which left four Imperial swordsman between Heros and the commander.

"Do you have a *name*, commander?" Heros asked.

"One the likes of *you* will never hear." The commander answered.

"Then I will simply call you 'Atrox'." Heros said.

"You have not yet experienced *true* atrocity." Atrox said.

"I have experienced *tyranny*, that *is* true atrocity." Heros said.

The remaining swordsman, who were huddled, glanced around the area.

"Why would *we* have to die to protect the commander?" An Imperial Swordsman said.

"Is tyranny making people die to protect people who do not deserve protection?" Another Imperial Swordsman asked.

"Betray the Empire and death will not be a *risk*; it will be a *certainty*." Atrox answered.

"So the choices are: die *protecting* tyranny, or die to *overthrow* tyranny? We know which one *you* chose, 'Atrox.'" The first of the Imperial Swordsmen to speak said.

"Then *die*, but tyranny will endure." Atrox said.

Atrox stabbed the Imperial swordsman who had dared to suggest overthrowing tyranny.

"It would seem 'Atrox' was indeed a rather apt name." Scorpio said.

"I would kill the Emperor slowly and painfully if I could, but I am a realist – tyranny will not go away while *I* am alive." Atrox said.

"The commander has a semblance of a *conscience*, it seems." Heros said.

"Perhaps, but *I* alone cannot overthrow a tyrant." Atrox said.

"Who said anything about overthrowing a tyrant by *yourself*?" Heros said.

The three remaining swordsmen pondered.

"If we *protect* tyranny, we will die, if we try to *overthrow* tyranny, we will die, if we *flee*, we will die, but maybe a little later. Men, how do you want to die?" A third swordsman who had not previously spoken said.

"I cannot defeat the magician alone." Atrox said.

"You could not defeat the magician even *with* our help. Men, if we flee, at least the Empire has to *find* us before they can *kill* us." The Third Swordsman said.

"If I find the three of you, I will make sure your corpses are incinerated." Atrox said.

"How do you plan to find us when you cannot even find a way of defeating the magician?" The Second Swordsman said.

The three surviving Imperial swordsmen fled. Scorpio slowly approached Atrox.

"Would you decline a *third* chance to surrender?" Heros asked.

"I would decline thirty chances to surrender if it is to someone who requires spirits to fight for him." Atrox said.

"Do you truly think you have seen my full arsenal of magic?" Heros asked.

"I have seen enough to know you must be *serious* about freeing the prisoners." Atrox answered.

"At what point did you *doubt* I was serious about freeing the prisoners?" Heros asked.

"I hope there is a hell *terrible* enough for your treachery." Atrox answered.

"If I go there, I hope to at least see *Emperor Colubrifer* there." Heros said.

"If the gods will it." Atrox said.

"I would like to think the gods do not will tyranny." Heros said.

"It is at least clear the gods do not will love and mercy, or we would have had no reason to invent that Deus Benevolus nonsense." Atrox said.

"It is not too late for you to keep your dignity even in

death. While you *deserve* a slow and painful death, you may pray that Deus Benevolus eases your passing." Heros said.

"Keep my dignity even in death, you say? Very well, I *shall*." Atrox said.

Atrox extended his arms by his sides and gestured for Heros to oblige him.

"Scorpio, make it a quick, clean kill. May Deus Benevolus guide you." Heros said.

Scorpio concentrated, then struck Atrox with his stinger. Scorpio's stinger appeared to glow, and Atrox was killed on impact.

"If belief in Deus Benevolus instils *mercy* in us, it is not 'nonsense'." Heros said.

"Shall we proceed to free the prisoners?" Scorpio asked.

"We shall." Heros answered.

Heros and Scorpio began to enter the internment camp.

Inside the prison part of the internment camp, Cetin prisoners spoke amongst themselves in Ketin. Heros and Scorpio began approaching the prisoners. Heros stopped, looked up, and remembered Sagittarius was still present.

"Thank you, Sagittarius, you are dismissed for now." Heros said.

"It was an honour to inflict an injury on tyranny." Sagittarius said.

Sagittarius glowed then vanished.

"We inflicted an injury on tyranny, you say? Probably a flesh wound at best." Heros said.

The Cetin prisoners seemed intimidated by Heros.

"Scorpio, how do I tell them I mean them no harm?" Heros asked.

"Find a way of speaking the same language first." Scorpio answered.

"Is there a translator among you?" Heros asked.

A non-emaciated female Cetin with white hair stepped forward.

"What would you have me tell the prisoners?" The Female Cetin asked.

"Rejoice, for your freedom is at hand." Heros answered.

The Female Cetin spoke in Ketin, then the group of Cetin prisoners, numbering perhaps a hundred, looked expectantly at Heros.

"How is it you can offer *us* freedom and yet do so little to offer your *own* people the same?" The Female Cetin asked.

"One man alone does not defeat tyranny." Heros answered.

"Unless that man is a *rather fortunate* assassin." The Female Cetin said.

"Unless such an assassin is rather unlikely to exist." Heros said.

"What have you to gain from *our* freedom?" The Female Cetin asked.

"There is more to lose by *not* freeing you." Heros answered.

The Female Cetin spoke several sentences in Ketin.

"The Cetin look forward to your people's freedom from tyranny." The Female Cetin said.

"It is not safe to celebrate until the Emperor's corpse is paraded down the streets." Heros said.

"Well said. Grant us safe passage back to Cetin territory and the Emperor might become a corpse *sooner* than you think." Heros said.

"But several decades ago, the Verian Empire *conquered* Cetin territories!" Heros said.

"You mostly conquered in the *south*, and you seemed more interested in filling these horrendous internment camps than conquering the *north*." The Female Cetin said.

"Even still, whatever plans the Cetin may have, you would need *great* confidence in the success of those plans, else you are deluding yourselves." Heros said.

"Before you succeeded at capturing this camp, did you not stop to think, perhaps, you might have been deluding *yourself*?" The Female Cetin asked.

"Which of you want *freedom*?" Heros shouted.

"Allow me to translate." The Female Cetin said.

The Female Cetin spoke a single sentence in Ketin. Of the emaciated prisoners, those with sufficient strength raised a fist.

"It seems freedom has the same meaning even in *your* language." Heros said.

A male Cetin prisoner spoke in Ketin.

"What is to become of this prison?" The Female Cetin asked.

"Maybe one day a tyrant will beg for his *freedom* here." Heros answered.

The Female Cetin translated into Ketin.

"If that is not too good for the likes of *him*." The Female Cetin said.

"*I* am not the mythical 'rather fortunate assassin' you mentioned. The Empire will shortly recover from the 'injury' I inflicted here." Heros said.

"Then your empire needs to be injured more *severely*." The Female Cetin said.

"When will you tell me your plans? If you will not, at least tell me your *name*." Heros said.

"For your protection, we should never meet again after this group has returned to Cetin territories." The Female Cetin said.

"I do not know how you plan to injure the Empire 'more severely', but may it be possible." Heros said.

"Heros, you will need to keep a low-profile after what we have done *here*." Scorpio said.

"There is not even a slight possibility I might *join* you when you return?" Heros asked.

"Do you think *our* lands will be safer than your *own* people's lands?" The Female Cetin answered.

"Would that notion be mistaken?" Heros asked.

"Not entirely." The Female Cetin answered.

HANDS THAT CANNOT GRIP
THE SANDS OF POWER

Arundineus and Caelifer were standing on a balcony somewhere in Magna Gloria.

"Did you hear a certain new rumour?" Caelifer asked.

"At any point in time, there are probably *hundreds* of rumours floating around the empire – *which* rumour am I supposed to have heard?" Arundineus answered.

"Rumours *float*, do they? Well, *Legionnaires* have been known to do that, so why not rumours?" Caelifer said.

"Would it kill you to get to the point instead of making jokes?" Arundineus asked.

"It *might*, who can say? There is a rumour one of the internment camps was attacked and all of the Cetin held there were freed. There is an even more *dubious* rumour that the person who attacked the internment camp was a magician." Caelifer answered.

"If I had been there with Legionaire…" Arundineus said.

"Let me see if I understand. You would have *opposed* the person who opposed tyranny?" Caelifer said.

"There is a difference between opposing tyranny and

helping the enemy." Arundineus said.

"In the Cetin's case, opposing tyranny makes them *less* of an enemy, if anything." Caelifer said.

Suddenly, a large group consisting of an equal number of imperial legionnaires and imperial archers ran past the balcony. One legionnaire broke off from the group, ran towards Arundineus and Caelifer, then stopped a short distance away from them.

"Arundineus Vulgatus, Caelifer Credo, assuming I have the correct people, our glorious emperor requests your immediate presence." The legionnaire said.

"*Glorious* emperor? Of course! No doubt *some* will find his contributions to *tyranny* glorious." Caelifer thought.

"What difference will *two* more people make?" Arundineus asked.

"Questioning the emperor could be the last thing you ever do." The legionnaire answered.

"That must make it hard to teach the emperor *mathematics*." Caelifer thought.

"Can you escort us to the imperial palace?" Arundineus asked.

"It is best not to keep the emperor waiting. Age has made him less tolerant." The legionnaire answered.

"He was barely *tolerant* to begin with, now he is simply *intolerable*." Caelifer thought.

The legionnaire bowed.

"Very well. I shall lead you to the imperial palace." The legionnaire said.

The group soon arrived at the imperial palace and entered the throne room. The Emperor, old and feeble, squinted to see who was with him in the room.

"Is that Arundineus and Caelifer?" Emperor Colubrifer asked.

"Was there not a matter of some urgency?" Arundineus answered.

"There often *is*. In the capital, as well as some uncooperative southern cities, there appears to be growing unrest." Emperor Colubrifer said.

"And likely, a growing sense the empire would be better off with *you* dead." Caelifer thought.

"The two of us would not be nearly enough to quell unrest." Arundineus said.

"Could you not quell the unrest with the help of Legionaire?" Emperor Colubrifer asked.

"Knowing *you*, it will have to be *brutal* in some way. Asking you what the opposite of brutal is would be a waste of time." Caelifer thought.

"Would you not want to minimise the number of casualties, Emperor Colubrifer?" Arundineus asked.

"Either you have not figured him out yet, or you are *deliberately* playing dumb." Caelifer thought.

"What do I care if some *traitors* are killed?" Emperor Colubrifer asked.

"*You* would not lose any sleep even if you ordered a massacre. Somnus's ability to give people bad dreams seems rather…*unreliable*." Caelifer thought.

"Your mysterious power – could that not be used to subdue traitors *instead*?" Emperor Colubrifer asked.

"My mysterious power – I think we have started calling it 'Outburst' – I cannot control it at will." Arundineus answered.

"Unfortunate. Very unfortunate." Emperor Colubrifer said.

"Has Arundineus outlived his usefulness to you *already*? 'Unfortunate' is the fact that you ruled as a tyrant for *forty five years too long*." Caelifer thought.

"Urbs Gravis seems to be the source of the unrest." Emperor Colubrifer said.

"I hear the nearby Lacuna Gravis is beautiful. Hopefully the lacuna will not run red with blood." Arundineus said.

"To *him*, a lacuna running red with blood probably *would* be beautiful." Caelifer thought.

"No, I would not pollute a beautiful lacuna in such a way. The corpses would be piled on the streets. Better that the *streets* run red with blood than the *lacuna*." Emperor Colubrifer said.

"The world needed no more proof of your insanity – it got more proof *anyway*." Caelifer thought.

"How did I ever manage to have *respect* for you?" Arundineus thought.

"The Empire is seemingly never safe from traitors." Emperor Colubrifer said.

"So all it takes for you to lose sleep is a little unrest and hints of an uprising? I am glad to *know* that." Caelifer thought.

"Even if there *are* traitors, surely they could be *imprisoned* instead of killed?" Arundineus said.

"There are not enough prisons in the entire empire to do so." Emperor Colubrifer said.

"Apparently, our long-reigning tyrant believes the empire does not have enough prisons. As long as there is one waiting for *you*, there *are* enough. Are there too few *internment camps* in your view as well?" Caelifer thought.

"In any case, solve the problem in Urbs Gravis or perhaps I might have *you* imprisoned." Emperor Colubrifer said.

"Who do we talk to about solving the problem of *being ruled by a tyrant*?" Caelifer thought.

"If those are your orders, Emperor. I do not know how you expect to minimise casualties." Arundineus said.

"He has no *expectation* of minimising casualties in the first place – surely you *knew* that?" Caelifer thought.

"When you arrive in Urbs Gravis, you are to relay new orders to my men. I would like to clear out some Cetin towns and expand our territory." Emperor Colubrifer said.

"See? If anything, he wants to *increase* casualties." Caelifer thought.

"Yes, Emperor, I will remember that." Arundineus said.

"You will remember there are more layers to Emperor Colubrifer's tyranny onion than you *thought*." Caelifer thought.

"That is all. You will be informed of any further orders." Emperor Colubrifer said.

"He wants *more* conflict with the Cetin? The Verian

military is not invincible, neither is the empire." Arundineus thought.

"Is there anything on your mind I should know about?" Emperor Colubrifer asked.

"You are asking the *wrong* person, believe me." Caelifer thought.

"Nothing of concern, Emperor." Arundineus said.

"Good. I was running out of patience for that unrest to go away *before* you came here." Emperor Colubrifer said.

Possibly up to a few days later, Arundineus and Caelifer arrived in Urbs Gravis. The town was of a considerable size, and in the distance was a large lake, Lacuna Gravis. A group of legionnaires and imperial archers were gathered near the town's western entrance. Arundineus and Caelifer approached them.

"Arundineus Vulgatus and Caelifer Credo, sent by the Emperor himself." Arundineus said.

"I cannot be completely sure you are not imposters, but you match the descriptions we were given." A legionnaire said.

"If only there was a way of creating an accurate depiction of what people look like." Caelifer said.

"The Empire would work on *inventing* it if we actually knew what you were *talking* about." The legionnaire said.

"You have new orders from the Emperor. Once the unrest is over, he wants to clear out some Cetin towns and capture them to expand our territory." Arundineus said.

"I would rather poke myself in the eye with my sword

than follow orders like *those*." The legionnaire said.

"You had better not let the *Emperor* find out you said that." Caelifer thought.

"It is true during that invasion of Cetin territories, once we captured many of the southern towns and returned to the Empire with Cetin prisoners, we did not leave behind forces anywhere near strong enough to permanently occupy the land we captured. However, the Cetin were caught off-guard, if we attack them again, they might be *expecting* us." The legionnaire said.

"One would wonder how, with such an extensive spy network, the Cetin *could* have been caught off-guard by an invasion." Caelifer said.

"We are not paid to speculate." The legionnaire said.

"Neither am *I*, but clearly *that* did not stop me." Caelifer said.

"How bad is the unrest here in Urbs Gravis?" Arundineus asked.

"It is not only *here*, but also in several other towns. Perhaps tyranny has a limited lifespan after all." The legionnaire answered.

"What do you mean 'after all'? Would not tyranny have a lifespan tied to the lifespan of the tyrant in question?" Caelifer thought.

"The Emperor wants the unrest quelled *brutally*." Arundineus said.

"You would think brutality was some kind of science the Emperor had yet to figure out." The legionnaire said.

"He obviously has yet to figure out that tyranny is a *bad idea*." Caelifer thought.

"How will we proceed with quelling the unrest?" Arundineus asked.

"The group here, we will scout the vicinity of Urbs Gravis, Lacuna Gravis and the surrounding area. Anyone who takes up arms against you is a traitor, and I assume the Emperor will not lose any sleep if those people are killed." The legionnaire said.

"Suppose someone *wanted* the Emperor to lose sleep, do you think an *uprising* might be enough?" Caelifer asked.

"Suppose you wanted to *lose your life*; do you think *telling jokes at the Emperor's expense* might be enough?" The legionnaire answered.

Caelifer smiled.

"He has me *there*." Caelifer said.

"Is now the proper time to be joking?" Arundineus asked.

"Never mind *him*, his sense of humour is *less developed* than mine." Caelifer answered.

"We shall proceed with the scouting when you are ready." The legionnaire said.

"Does that mean if we never admit to being ready, the supposed traitors will not lose their lives?" Caelifer asked.

"If you attempt to stall us, we shall proceed without you, and also proceed to inform the Emperor of your disobedience." The legionnaire answered.

"Now seems like as good a time as any to get started.

What do you *think*, Arundineus?" Caelifer said.

"I could hardly agree more with that first sentence." Arundineus said.

"What was wrong with the *second* of those two sentences?" Caelifer thought.

The group of imperial soldiers cautiously began entering Urbs Gravis. There were few obvious signs of unrest.

"This might sound stupid, but should there not be more signs of unrest?" Arundineus asked.

"Sounding stupid is a worry I stopped paying attention to *long* ago." Caelifer answered.

"The townspeople might be spread out – some are probably in their homes, and I suspect many of them have prepared an ambush in the area surrounding the town." The legionnaire said.

"So we should be worried about the ones we *cannot* see?" Arundineus asked.

"Exactly. To the south and east of the town, I suspect they have planned an ambush." The legionnaire answered.

"Surely not *all* of the townspeople are traitors?" Arundineus asked.

"Babies and very young children, probably not." The legionnaire answered.

"How is a baby only *probably* not a traitor?" Caelifer thought.

"How comforting. What is the rough population of Urbs Gravis?" Arundineus asked.

"Population? Roughly about…" The legionnaire answered.

Suddenly, an arrow was shot from inside one of the houses and struck a legionnaire in the torso. Several other arrows were shot from inside other houses. A small number of enemy arrows missed, but most struck either an imperial legionnaire or an imperial archer. About half of the imperial soldiers present were struck by an arrow.

"Defend yourselves! Our enemy is hiding in plain sight!" The legionnaire said.

The imperial forces assumed defensive positions.

"A little *arson* would probably be persuasive." Caelifer said.

"Is it not a little late for that?" The legionnaire asked.

"We talk about 'the fires of war', do nothing to prevent that arson, and then complain about the mere *suggestion* of arson? That might be something called *hypocrisy*." Caelifer answered.

"We would at least need some rocks to create a spark." The legionnaire said.

"You are not already enough of a spark *yourself*?" Caelifer asked.

"It is almost as though the enemy *expected* us. We would need at least *twice* as many men to raid the houses." The legionnaire answered.

"Unless we could devise an effective distraction." Arundineus said.

"Three times as many men arriving from the east?! It is almost as though these paltry forces were just to test the enemy's strength." Caelifer shouted.

"What are you *doing*?" Arundineus asked in a whisper.

"Would *that* suffice as a distraction?" Caelifer answered.

"Would the enemy *fall* for that?" Arundineus asked.

"Look at *you* – already calling those who oppose tyranny 'the enemy'." Caelifer answered.

"I prefer calling them 'the enemy' to calling them traitors. Anyone who *supports* tyranny is a *true* traitor." Arundineus said.

"The enemy has not fallen for our distraction." The legionnaire said.

"Maybe they need more time to consider their options." Arundineus said.

"'Anyone who supports tyranny is a true traitor.' Thank the gods, there is still some *hope* for you." Caelifer thought.

Some of the enemy archers inside the houses cautiously peeked out into the town. Suddenly, several enemy archers fled from the houses they had sheltered in and ran directly south. The remaining enemy archers soon followed. The enemy archers ran towards the southern part of the town.

"Leave no survivors!" The legionnaire said.

"They set a trap! Defend yourselves!" One of the enemy archers said.

The imperial archers and enemy archers engaged each other. Meanwhile, imperial legionnaires began to approach enemy archers wherever it was safe enough to approach them.

"If you let a legionnaire reach you, you are as good as dead." Another enemy archer said.

"'As good as dead' will be the population of this town." Caelifer thought.

Several imperial legionnaires were closing in on enemy archers. The affected archers frantically shot approaching legionnaires, taking down most of them. A small number of the affected archers, though succeeding in eliminating an approaching legionnaire, were hit by imperial archers in the confusion. About half the enemy archers remained, and the imperial archers now outnumbered them.

"How can you serve an insane tyrant?" Yet another enemy archer asked.

"The consequences for *refusing* to serve are too great." The legionnaire answered.

"The consequences for refusing to *overthrow tyranny* are too great." The enemy archer said.

"*You* should be leading a rebel army. How has no one *recruited* you?" Caelifer thought.

Suddenly, an arrow from an enemy archer approached Arundineus, but perhaps a split second before it connected, Arundineus's so-called 'Outburst' power activated, and the arrow hit his torso and was deflected.

"If we had *fifty* men like that…" The legionnaire said.

"Until now, you probably did not even know the Empire had *one* man like that." Caelifer said.

Arundineus ran towards the nearest enemy archers and engaged them in close combat. He defeated about five archers in close succession, but then his Outburst power began to falter. There was a pause to the fighting.

"How soon will it be until he can do that *again*?" The legionnaire asked.

"We know very little about Arundineus's so-called Outburst ability. We are not even entirely sure if Outburst is a *good name* for it." Caelifer answered.

The enemy archers appeared unsure what to make of Outburst, and were reluctant to keep fighting.

"If they surrender, this need not be a bloodbath." Arundineus said.

"It *need* be not a bloodbath, but a certain Emperor probably *wants* it to be." Caelifer thought.

"I am not sure if the Emperor would approve." The legionnaire said.

"Wipe an entire town off the map because of a hint of unrest – what sane person would approve of *that*?" Caelifer thought.

"The one who turned red…his ability seems unreliable." An enemy archer said.

"He looks vulnerable – should we eliminate him?" Another enemy archer asked.

"There should have been a way to resolve all this peacefully. I will not participate in a bloodbath." Arundineus said.

"'I will not participate in a bloodbath' – *Emperor Snake-mouth* would never say that. 'I *order* a bloodbath' is something he might say, though." Caelifer thought.

"What are our options at this point?" A third enemy archer asked.

"If we flee, we have a lower chance of dying." A fourth

enemy archer answered.

"If they had brought three times as many men to *begin with*, they could have easily raided the houses. Do not underestimate those enslaved by the Empire." The first archer said.

"'Those enslaved by the Empire' – with tyranny, *the general population*." Caelifer thought.

"Better that we die *free*." The fourth archer said.

The remaining enemy archers fled south. Arundineus gestured to the legionnaire.

"Let them go. No one in this town should die needlessly." Arundineus said.

"I would go further and say no one *at all* should die needlessly." Caelifer said.

"An impossible ideal. A *noble* ideal, but a *foolish* one." The legionnaire said.

"Ideals *themselves* might be foolish. Call me a foolish idealist if you wish." Caelifer said.

"Why would I wish to do *that*?" The legionnaire asked.

"Perhaps to appear wise by criticising a fool?" Caelifer answered.

"You are rather wise for a *fool*, then, Caelifer." Arundineus thought.

"If *I* had magical arrow-deflecting powers like Arundineus, I would have charged against those archers *myself*." The legionnaire said.

"Where is the supposed *ambush* you were so afraid of?" Caelifer asked.

"The emperor would want the enemy's heads." The legionnaire answered.

"Anyone opposing tyranny would want the *Emperor's* head...if they ever manage to *obtain* it, sell it to the highest bidder." Caelifer thought.

Caelifer could barely prevent himself from smiling with amusement.

"What is *he* so happy about?" The legionnaire asked.

"I would rather not say." Arundineus answered.

One enemy archer had refused to flee, and took aim at the legionnaire.

"If I kill *one* cowardly servant of tyranny, my life will have had meaning." The enemy archer said.

"What will 'a life for a life' achieve?" Arundineus asked.

"Obviously enough for him to consider it worthwhile to throw away *his*." Caelifer answered.

"How can you put so little value on your own life?" Arundineus asked.

"How can you put so much effort into *defending tyranny*?" The enemy archer answered.

"He has us *there*!" Caelifer said.

"On second thought, perhaps if I kill the man with the power to deflect arrows instead." The enemy archer said.

The enemy archer took aim at Arundineus.

"No, stop it!" Arundineus shouted.

Suddenly, Outburst activated and a red dagger materialised and flew at the enemy archer. The enemy archer fell to his knees.

"What god gave you such power?" The enemy archer asked.

The enemy archer collapsed and began bleeding out.

"Shall we return and report to the Emperor?" Arundineus asked.

"You say it like we actually have any choice in the matter." Caelifer answered.

"Choice is something the Emperor considers an inconvenience." The legionnaire said.

Arundineus, the legionnaire and Caelifer were standing before the Emperor in the throne room of the imperial palace.

"We have returned from Urbs Gravis, Emperor." The legionnaire said.

"How fared your men? How many survived?" Emperor Colubrifer asked.

"Over half of my men survived. When we arrived, the enemy was taking shelter inside houses. We considered committing arson, but we lacked a method of creating a flame." The legionnaire said.

"Arson…I like the *sound* of that." Emperor Colubrifer said.

"The last thing we need is *you* getting bad ideas. *You* getting bad ideas I do *not* like the sound of." Caelifer thought.

"Burn Urbs Gravis completely to the ground. An example shall be made of them." Emperor Colubrifer said.

"Is that truly *necessary*, Emperor?" The legionnaire asked.

"*I* decide what is necessary! You *dare* question your Emperor?" Emperor Colubrifer answered.

"'Necessary' is *you* being removed from power, preferably as soon as possible." Caelifer thought.

"I only question the necessity of burning a town that we have already captured." The legionnaire said.

Emperor Colubrifer smirked. In his advanced age, his face smirking appeared hideous.

"Very well, then you are ordered to burn whichever the next town to rebel is. Failure to obey will result in your prompt execution." Emperor Colubrifer said.

"Things like *that* are why tyranny *does not work*." Caelifer thought.

"As you wish, Emperor. It is not worth risking execution for." The legionnaire said.

"When will those foolish traitors realise creating unrest could get them *killed*?" Emperor Colubrifer said.

"What glory did *you* ever bring to the Empire? Overthrowing tyranny *would* be worth risking execution for." Caelifer thought.

"Have you any further orders, Emperor?" The legionnaire asked.

"If only I had." Emperor Colubrifer answered.

"If only you had *died when we fought Selene*." Caelifer thought.

"Come along, Caelifer, before you get any ideas." The legionnaire said.

"Far too *late* for that." Caelifer said.

A MAJESTIC FALL

Several months passed. Far from dying down, unrest continued in some parts of the empire, including the capital. The empire's army was stretched thin in order to impose some measure of control in the chaos of the unrest. A vast Cetin fleet, as many as 250 ships, arrived near the northwest coast of the Cunaea continent. Imperial coastal defences capable of repelling the Cetin fleet were not available.

Several days later, Arundineus, Caelifer and Pugna were in the imperial throne room before Emperor Colubrifer.

"Curse those Cetin demons!" Emperor Colubrifer said.

"What terrible thing have they done, Emperor?" Arundineus asked.

"A Cetin fleet of at least two hundred and fifty ships approached the northwest coast of Cunaea, and Cetin forces have been steadily approaching the capital." Emperor Colubrifer answered.

"Have you not sent forces to stall them?" Arundineus asked.

"The Cetin cleverly timed their invasion to coincide with the recent unrest. There are barely any forces to spare lest unrest be ignored at the empire's peril. That is the first and *only* time you will hear me praise Cetin for their clever-ness." Emperor Colubrifer answered.

"I suspect 'clever' is not a word much used to describe tyrants. You should stick with 'cruel' or 'ruthless'." Caelifer thought.

"The three of us cannot defeat an entire army." Arundineus said.

"Surely you and Legionaire can at least hinder the Cetin army's progress for a short time?" Emperor Colubrifer asked.

"Perhaps, but they would still eventually reach the capital." Arundineus answered.

"Curse those demons for knowing when we were most vulnerable!" Emperor Colubrifer said.

"We will hinder the enemy as best we can. There will be a bloodbath." Arundineus said.

"Then a bloodbath there shall *be*." Emperor Colubrifer said.

Some time later, Arundineus, Caelifer and Pugna reached the imperial frontline. Legionaire was present. An overwhelming number of Cetin were approaching the capital. About five hundred imperials were present.

"Arundineus, in case we do not survive, your love elevated me, I learned…" Pugna said.

"I could have sworn romantic discussions were a *private* subject." Caelifer said.

"Pugna, if you resent me for choosing to not have children, take out all your resentment on me *now* in case we do not survive this battle." Arundineus said.

"What if you do not survive my resentment?" Pugna asked.

"If you two are still together, clearly he already *has* survived your resentment." Caelifer said.

A nearby legionnaire approached.

"The enemy is estimated to number at least twenty five thousand." The legionnaire said.

"One hundred enemies per ship…*impressive*." Pugna said.

"Even if Legionaire and I kill a thousand enemies between us, Magna Gloria will *still* be doomed." Arundineus said.

"Pity Sol Invictus is not some god who can incinerate enemies with sunlight. Maybe pray to him *anyway*, in case I am wrong." Caelifer said.

"At least you are not wrong to have a sense of humour." Arundineus thought.

A wave of enemies began closing in. About 4/5 of the enemies were archers, and the remaining 1/5 were armed with melee weapons. The Cetin archers began taking aim.

"When you are ready, Legionaire, we give them *hell*!" Arundineus said.

"I was waiting for *you*." Legionaire said.

"Defender of the Legion!" Arundineus shouted.

A magical shield appeared around the front-most row of imperial soldiers.

"Our enemies are legion, but I shall defend the empire even if it avails little." Legionaire said.

The Cetin archers attacked, while some of the Cetin melee fighters approached the magically-shielded front row of imperials. Pugna scored some impressive shots.

"Such strength and tenacity, even at *her* age." Arundineus thought.

"Legionaire, kill as many of the green-skinned men as possible." Arundineus said.

"Very well, but do not neglect your own defence." Legionaire said.

"Shield of the Legion!" Arundineus shouted.

A magical shield appeared around Arundineus.

"Now, shall we give them *hell*?" Legionaire said.

Arundineus and Legionaire ploughed through the nearest group of Cetin enemies. Legionaire used Empire Slash, Empire Thrust and Empire Slice instinctively, without being instructed. In mere moments, about fifty Cetin were killed as a direct result of Arundineus's and Legionaire's teamwork.

"Legionaire, can Defender of the Legion protect the rest of our forces here?" Arundineus asked.

"It is not even intended to protect as many as that front row." Legionaire answered.

"That sounds like a *no*." Caelifer said.

The front-most row of imperial forces fought fiercely, and the combined imperial forces present managed to kill seventy or more Cetin, with little to no visible decrease in the enemy's numbers.

"Fight not for yourself, fight to protect the empire!"

Arundineus shouted.

"It turns out the Cetin could somehow afford war *after all*. Have scholars made any progress figuring out the *Cetin economy* yet?" Caelifer said.

"To be humourous even in the face of almost certain death…how do you *do it*, Caelifer?" Pugna thought.

The magical shield protecting the front-most row of imperials began to falter.

"If Defender of the Legion stops working, the front row is finished." Arundineus said.

"I was not created to even such hopeless odds." Legionaire said.

"Or, to put it *another* way: how are we still alive and able to keep fighting?" Caelifer said.

"I am beginning to wonder about that *myself.*" Pugna said.

The Cetin forces launched a ferocious attack against the front-most row of imperial forces. The magical shield finally disappeared, and the front-most row began to weaken under relentless assault by the enemy.

"Legionaire, is there anything more you can do?" Arundineus asked.

"We are too severely outnumbered for anything I might suggest to be of true benefit." Legionaire answered.

"How is unrest a greater threat than an invasion? Arundineus, do *you* know?" Caelifer asked.

"I do not even know how Emperor Colubrifer evaded *assassins* for so long. There is much blood on my hands."

Arundineus answered.

"If there is a more than a drop of blood on your hands, the Emperor's hands are *drenched* with it." Caelifer said.

Most of the front-most row of imperials fell to relentless enemy attacks. The imperial forces were indeed scoring kills, but of far too insufficient numbers to have any direct effect on the battle.

"Are you starting to feel pain for having wronged us?" A Cetin soldier near Arundineus asked.

"Is revenge the only thing the Cetin *care* about now?" Arundineus asked.

"You have to suffer enough to think twice about wronging us in future." The Cetin soldier near Arundineus answered.

"I might have thought twice about *killing* you if the Emperor was your *only* target. Empire Slash!" Arundineus said.

Legionaire obeyed and the unlucky Cetin soldier was hit to the left of his torso, with his left arm cleanly sliced off.

"Is there…a…Creator?" The unlucky Cetin soldier managed to say before bleeding out.

"Arundineus, we cannot stall the Cetin indefinitely. Do we fight to the last person or retreat to the capital?" Pugna said.

"Maybe we bought time for some imperial forces to return to guard the capital…maybe." Arundineus said.

"Should we have surrendered and insisted on a peace treaty?" Pugna asked.

"And agree to a peace treaty on the *Cetin's* terms?"

Arundineus answered.

"What is so honourable about dying in battle?" Pugna asked.

"Having heroic poetry written about you supposedly has some kind of appeal. Dying on account of a tyrant is about as appealing as choosing to lie down on a bed of snakes." Caelifer answered.

"In *Colubrifer's* case, both choices sound the same." Arundineus said.

"And *I* am meant to be the humourous one." Caelifer said.

"Can someone please answer my question?" Pugna asked.

"A retreat is risky – we do not have enough forces to spare to cover our retreat." Arundineus said.

"We do not have enough forces to do more than irritate the enemy either." Caelifer said.

"*I* will slow the enemy's advance. I cannot *die*, after all." Legionaire said.

"But if a Cetin magician manages to…" Arundineus said.

"We have seen no enemy magicians among the invasion force. My presence at this battle must not have been anticipated." Legionaire said.

"*His* suggestion might save some lives." Pugna said.

Arundineus touched his forehead with his free hand.

"How much do you expect to slow the enemy down, Legionaire?" Arundineus asked.

"The gods alone might know." Legionaire answered.

"Send the enemy to Hell." Arundineus said.

Arundineus bowed.

"Imperial forces, retreat to Magna Gloria! We cannot stall the enemy much longer!" Arundineus shouted.

The imperial forces began a full retreat. Legionaire stood defiantly against the Cetin forces.

"Who is ready to go to Hell?" Legionaire asked.

Some time later, the retreating forces had returned to Magna Gloria. A small number of imperial forces awaited them, modestly bolstering their numbers.

"There is not much time. An evacuation of the capital is out of the question." Arundineus said.

"The imperial palace will be one of their first targets in the capital. As many men as we can spare should guard the imperial palace. Colubrifer may be a tyrant, but we will not make him an easy target for the enemy." Pugna said.

"If our archers can defend from higher ground, it might give us a slight advantage." Arundineus said.

"There is almost no doubt the capital will fall. The *important* question is: how long can we resist?" Pugna asked.

Some time later, perhaps a day or two, the Cetin forces closed in on the capital. Their numbers appeared essentially undiminished.

"Archers, the more enemies you kill, the more imperial lives are saved." Arundineus said.

"How many Cetin have we *actually* killed?" Pugna asked.

"Nowhere near enough to make much difference."

Caelifer said.

The imperial defences at the entrance to Magna Gloria fell within a few hours. Because most of the enemies were archers and only a fraction of them melee combatants, defending from higher ground provided only a small advantage.

"We will protect the imperial palace with our last breaths if we must." Pugna said.

"You want your last act to be *dying to protect a tyrant*? Why does tyranny bring out so much *insanity* in people?" Caelifer thought.

"I am not sure how effectively we will be *able* to protect the imperial palace." Arundineus said.

"And I am not sure that I *want* to. Tyranny should have died *long* ago." Arundineus thought.

Cetin forces began to flood the capital.

"Even if Sol Invictus *could* incinerate enemies with sunlight, what if *we* were not protected from that?" Caelifer said.

"Did the Cetin have a hand in the recent unrest in the empire? How long was this invasion *planned*?" Arundineus said.

"Wondering about things like *those* at times like *these* is enough to get you killed." Caelifer said.

"The gods could not have wanted to see Magna Gloria in ruins, *could* they?" Pugna asked.

"I think about the *gods* about as much as I think about *reasons why having a sense of humour is a bad idea.*" Caelifer answered.

Pugna appeared puzzled.

"In other words, very little indeed." Arundineus said.

"Having a sense of humour *about* the gods might not be such a bad idea, though." Pugna said.

"I have already *thought* about that, *believe* me." Caelifer said.

The Cetin were beginning to swarm the far west of the capital. There was no hope of repelling the invasion.

A group of five male Cetin burst into the throne room. One of them was very muscular and wielded a large axe. Emperor Colubrifer stood and got on the floor on all fours. The group of male Cetin approached Emperor Colubrifer.

"Today we get to kill a tyrant. Now is the time to start believing in *generous* gods!" The axe-wielding Cetin male said.

"I beg you, spare my life! I will abdicate, here and now, I swear it!" Emperor Colubrifer said.

"My men here would be very disappointed if we left without killing a tyrant after I just praised the gods for *giving* us such an opportunity in the first place." The axe-wielding Cetin male said.

"I abdicate, it is done. Put a Cetin puppet on the Verian throne, if only you will *spare* me." Emperor Colubrifer said.

"What do you say, men? Let the Emperor live, or kill a tyrant?" The axe-wielding Cetin male said.

"Kill a tyrant!" The four other members of the Cetin group said in unison.

"My men have spoken. We will not be leaving disappointed

at all." The axe-wielding Cetin male said.

The axe-wielding Cetin male approached Emperor Colubrifer. Two of his fellow Cetin restrained Colubrifer. The axe-wielding Cetin male used his axe to behead Emperor Colubrifer.

"One of you remember to collect his head, we ought not return home without his head." The axe-wielding Cetin male said.

"For *proof* or as a *trophy*?" One of the other four Cetin in the group asked.

"I would assume both. Even some of the *humans* would celebrate tyranny's *glorious demise.*" The axe-wielding Cetin male said.

Arundineus, Caelifer and Pugna encountered the small Cetin group.

"How did our good emperor keep from *losing his head* for so long?" Caelifer asked.

"If you attempt to escape, *your* demise will be *equally* glorious." Pugna said.

"When word gets out the Emperor's head is waiting to be taken back to Megaleiodis, *others* will come for it, and perhaps, *your* demise might be celebrated." The axe-wielding Cetin male said.

"Is anyone here *actually* going to be killed, or should we let the Cetin figure out what to do with Colubrifer's head? Probably better than what *Colubrifer* was using it for in any case." Caelifer said.

"If you let us escape safely, we might guarantee your

capital is still able to be *recognised* when we are finished pillaging it." The axe-wielding Cetin male said.

"We have no proof you will keep your word." Pugna said.

"Five Cetin and the Emperor's head – a *small* price to save your capital from total ruin." Another member of the Cetin group said.

"Shall I kill this group of green-skinned men?" Legionaire asked.

"Legionaire? Where *are* you?" Arundineus thought.

"Have you forgotten already that I can conceal my appearance?" Legionaire asked.

"Killing that group of Cetin will be something that 'avails little', as you put it." Arundineus thought.

"Will the Emperor be granted no *dignity* in death?" Legionaire asked.

"It would seem not. I have *many* questions, Legionaire." Arundineus thought.

"Now is a time either for fighting or dying, not a time for seeking answers." Legionaire said.

"Is anyone going to say anything? This silence is vexing." Another of the Male Cetin said.

"Their capital has essentially already fallen. Leave them to lament their once-glorious empire." The axe-wielding Cetin male said.

The axe-wielding Cetin male began walking out of the throne room. He gestured for the rest of his group to follow.

"Kill us and hundreds more will avenge us. Farewell, Magna Gloria." The axe-wielding Cetin male said.

The group of five Cetin men left the throne room and began making their way out of the imperial palace.

"Is *this* how tyranny dies? A long, painful gasp?" Pugna asked.

"I wanted to see the Snake Emperor die more than anyone, but not like *this*. It seems I got my wish of him being beheaded, after all." Caelifer answered.

"The Verian people can never again afford a tyrant to gain power." Arundineus said.

"How many of 'the Verian people' will be *left* when the Cetin have finished with Magna Gloria?" Pugna asked.

"I hope going to such extraordinary lengths to quell unrest was *worth* it, Snake Emperor." Caelifer answered.

"You cannot possibly *mean* that." Arundineus said.

"Mean to be sarcastic? I possibly *can*." Caelifer said.

"While we are being sarcastic, I hope *revenge* was worth enough to the Cetin to cause so much *death*." Arundineus said.

"What if it was *not*?" Pugna asked.

"Then may the gods help anyone foolish enough to *annoy* the Cetin." Arundineus answered.

Several days later, the Cetin had captured Magna Gloria, and there was still some intermittent pillaging, and a small pockets of fighting within the capital. Arundineus, Caelifer and Pugna inspected the moderately ruined capital from a balcony. The capital was still recognisable, barely.

"The gods could have *warned* us annoying the Cetin would have such severe consequences." Pugna said.

"The gods could do *many* things; we mortals can never be entirely sure they are doing *any* of them." Caelifer said.

"Perhaps we mortals can never be entirely sure of much *at all*." Arundineus said.

"Did that group of Cetin keep their word *after all*?" Pugna asked.

"We will probably never be entirely sure." Caelifer answered.

Arundineus and Pugna laughed.

"You are probably *correct*. What are we mortals *actually* entirely sure of?" Arundineus said.

"Is that question even worth answering?" Caelifer said.

"What is to become of the Verian Empire? A Verian *Republic* bearing a *Cetin* flag?" Pugna asked.

"Or worse, a Verian Republic with a line of Cetin rulers. Subjugation by the enemy is barely any better than *tyranny*." Arundineus answered.

"What do you mean 'better'? Subjugation by an enemy is not much *different* to tyranny. Whoever disagrees must truly *hate* freedom." Caelifer said.

"I would pity those who would hate *freedom*." Arundineus said.

"I worry for the future." Pugna said.

"I know what you mean. What sane person would trade *tyranny* for *subjugation*?" Caelifer said.

"I mean, many years from now. Perhaps hundreds of years from now. Will our people's relations with the Cetin be any better than ours *now*? What if they are *worse*?" Pugna asked.

"Has someone already forgotten our discussion regarding *not being entirely sure*?" Caelifer answered.

"Will the future be *brighter* or *dimmer* than now?" Pugna asked.

"The future will be whatever it will be, we cannot know anything about the future with certainty *beyond* that." Arundineus said.

"The most accurate prediction I have ever *heard*." Caelifer said.

"Arundineus Vulgatus, the Verian Empire's most accurate *fortune-teller*." Pugna said.

"A title I *reluctantly* accept." Arundineus said.

"What if not even the *gods* know the future?" Pugna asked.

"Then who *does*? Unless what a Cetin on the battlefield said is true, unless there is some kind of Creator. That is, if it is even *possible* to know the future." Arundineus answered.

"*Another* accurate prediction: the three of us will *die* before too long." Caelifer said.

"We probably *will*, in which case, I hope there *is* a Creator. Perhaps Deus Benevolus is that very Creator." Arundineus said.

"He would *have* to be to be powerful enough to be a deity renowned for His *benevolence*. No *minor* god could make claim to such benevolence." Pugna said.

"Then why the pretence of him *being* some minor god?" Arundineus asked.

"How long would it take people to accept that almost

everything they *think* they know about the gods is *wrong*?" Caelifer asked.

"In the future, people in our time might be considered proud fools." Arundineus answered.

"However proud they may be in the future, I doubt they will be as foolish." Caelifer said.

"Maybe in some ways, *more* foolish." Pugna said.

"May the gods, or a Creator, if there is one, forbid it." Arundineus said.

Later, Arundineus and Pugna were together at a market. Most of the market stalls were desperately low on stock.

"Arundineus, why did you keep choosing to not have children?" Pugna asked.

"I did not want to bring more people into a land ruled by tyranny. I would have denied them the choice to avoid being ruled by a tyrant to satisfy my own desire, and called it 'love'. That would have been *selfish*." Arundineus answered.

"If our land had *not* been ruled by tyranny?" Pugna asked.

"I might have *considered* having children. Was my choice *wrong*?" Arundineus answered.

"Perhaps Deus Benevolus has touched you." Pugna said.

"What did we come to the market for, again?" Arundineus asked.

"Is he trying to change the subject?" Pugna thought.

"The Cetin seemed more merciful than I expected." Pugna said.

"If they thought we could *defeat* them, I suspect they

would have been *much* less merciful." Arundineus said.

"Who do the *Cetin* believe in?" Pugna asked.

"Deus Benevolus would be too *gentle* for peoples like them." Arundineus answered.

"I have never seen the market so empty. Most of the shops have barely anything to sell." Pugna said.

"Hopefully the future will not know any atrocities worse than the Cetin invasion, and the tragedy of tyranny." Arundineus said.

"The Tragedy of Tyranny...a popular play yet to be performed." Pugna said.

"And one that will never be forgotten, if Deus Benevolus is kind." Arundineus said.

"Proof of such *kindness* is elusive." Pugna said.

"Perhaps the future will be kinder." Arundineus said.

"I suspect the future will have its *own* tragedies." Pugna said.

REFLECTING ON HISTORY

And so, Emperor Colubrifer was forcibly deposed and the fall of the Verian Empire became what is *now* history.

It is unfortunate that Colubrifer's tyranny was not necessarily something new to the Verian Empire, but direct conflict between humans and the Cetin *might* have been. Seeds were sown which now have long since grown into noxious blooms.

A period of instability followed directly after the Verian Empire's fall. The Cetin withdrew from the Verian capital, but this 'mercy' came at the cost of many years of high taxation paid to the Cetin.

"At least we had peace", some would remind us. Was it really peace though, or cleverly manipulated extortion? Peace we may have had, but not freedom.

It would be a simple matter to demonise the Cetin, but even we humans can sometimes exhibit behaviour not unlike a demon. Certainly, inner demons can be as much of an issue for we humans as with the Cetin – sadly, some humans can even be *more* demonic than even some of the vilest members of the Cetin race.

A mere few centuries after the Verian Empire's fall,

the notorious thousand-year conflict known as The Great Purge raged. However, it should be clarified that The Great Purge does not refer to a single war spanning a millennium – a common enough misconception – but refers instead to numerous *smaller* conflicts, and broken treaties and violated ceasefires were by no means unheard of.

For the sake of brevity, political assassinations, both those attempted as well as those that were successful, were more or less a fact of life. It seems political assassinations are a reality regardless of the era in question, and perhaps will *always* be a reality as long as beings susceptible to death exist, furthermore, perhaps murderers will always exist so long as there are beings susceptible to death. If either or both of those assumptions are true, then they are sad truths about our mortal plane.

The Verian Empire persisted for roughly a century after Colubrifer's death, at least in name – more a formality than on account of power or wealth.

Before the Eighth Century U.C.E was over, at a senate meeting, a destitute person on the streets outside the senate building began chanting the phrase 'Egens boo!'. Eventually a significant number of the poor gathered and joined the chanting.

A senator proposed the formation of a successor to the Verian Empire named The Eggyboo Republic. The proposal passed with overwhelming but not unanimous support in the senate.

The fledgeling republic was to be a fairer and more just

democracy, but how well it manages to be any of those three things, let alone all three, is debatable.

Something that is *not* debatable is that the number of misfortunes the Cetin have been blamed for is significantly greater than the number of misfortunes they were *actually* responsible for. The so-called 'Devil', if there even *is* one, has similarly been blamed for a multitude of misfortunes and in all likelihood is responsible for very few of them, if indeed he even exists to begin with.

Though it must be pointed out that the Cetin religion apparently worships some 'King of the Underworld', which does not exactly help the Cetin's case.

The Cetin religion is probably a much greater factor in the Cetin's plight than any kind of human aversion to horns. While we generally tolerate their religion, we neither accept nor understand it. There may be subtleties to Cetin religious beliefs that we do not fully understand, and perhaps, sometimes *neglect* to understand.

Conflict with the Cetin is not necessarily inevitable, though in less enlightened times, it might well have been. There have been times when we humans kicked the hornet's nest, and usually we find ourselves regretting it eventually. That is not to say there have not been significant military victories against the Cetin, but violence never brought lasting peace for us...or at least, any peace derived from conflict was usually short-lived.

The Eggyboo Republic is not the shining example of virtue many would like it to be but the Eggyboo Republic on a *bad* day is probably still better than the supposed 'glory days' of the Verian Empire.

The Eggyboo Republic has ideals – no shortage of ideals, in fact – but its citizens are often left disappointed when reality falls far short of ideals. The Cetin, on the other hand, more rarely trade in ideals and grudgingly accept reality – would that we could do likewise. Some would not deign to learn anything from the Cetin, not even grudgingly. Prejudice sometimes triumphs over pragmatism – "logic be damned", it would seem. If emotion sometimes triumphs over logic, the same must surely be true of prejudice and pragmatism.

Colubrifer's tyranny may seem almost *quaint* in our more enlightened times but with the right, er, *necessary* circumstances tyranny could theoretically take hold again. A truly modern tyranny would be disastrous, but not un-thinkable. Tyranny might well be yet another thing possible regardless of the era. If that is true, complacency is one of our greatest enemies and one we are not always properly equipped to fight.

Colubrifer was very much a snake in the grass – the signs should have been obvious, but perhaps the aforemen-tioned grass was unusually long and someone had forgotten to cut it. No evidence has been found to suggest snake bites were ever used as a form of punishment during Colubrifer's reign, hopefully disproving that unsettling notion, but then again, maybe archaeologists were simply not looking in the right places – an even *more* unsettling notion. Some scant evidence has been found of a snake motif, but it has not been proven to be from Colubrifer's reign, and even if it had been, was in rare usage. A fictionalised account of Colubrifer's reign would probably be more satisfying than reality anyway.

A curious legacy of the Verian Empire is the choice of the Eggyboo Republic to name its new currency 'Veriat', as though to make sure our Republic's origins were never in doubt, or for *that* matter, never forgotten. This legacy is given little acknowledgement, as though the population either gladly accepts it or otherwise could hardly care less about it. There has, of course, been much speculation on the significance of the letter 't' in the word 'Veriat' – it has even been suggested the 't' is short for token, but there is a lack of supporting evidence.

The future of Planets Asiyah and Yetzirah is not yet certain, but civilisation will last as long as our mortal plane, or God, perhaps, decides. Civilisation will continue, until it cannot. Let us hope, at least, that if civilisation becomes doomed, it is due to some unavoidable cosmic catastrophe and that civilisation will not be doomed by its *own* hand.

May we never give up hope for the future.

OTHER BOOKS BY THIS AUTHOR

Do you aspire to be a writer, but aren't sure where to start?
Then let this book give you a head-start! When you write stuff, hopefully it will be the right stuff!

From a reality check to manage your expectations of the creative industry, to valuable insight into writing scripts including video game scripts, advice to improve your writing, mistakes to avoid, and creative affirmations to boost your confidence. This book might not have everything, but it sure beats having nothing - 'nothing' isn't even a worthy opponent for this book!

If you're serious about creative writing, give this book serious consideration! If you plan to be a serious writer, then it's time to get serious! Fight to write better, you go-getter!

The Writer's Quick-Start Guide
by Brendan Lloyd. ISBN: 978-1-922788-30-6
www.vividpublishing.com.au/writersguide